OH
HEAVENLY DOG

OH HEAVENLY DOG

by
Joe Camp

based upon the screenplay
by
Rod Browning & Joe Camp

A Hippo Book
Scholastic Publications Limited
London

Twentieth Century-Fox
presents
A Mulberry Square Production
A Film by Joe Camp

Chevy Chase
and
Benji
are
OH HEAVENLY DOG

starring
Jane Seymour ★ Omar Sharif as Malcolm Bart

Guest Star
Robert Morley

also starring
Alan Sues ★ Donnelly Rhodes

ISBN: 0-590-72083-X

12 11 10 9 8 7 6 5 4 3 2 1   1   1 2 3 4 5/8
Commonwealth Edition
Printed in the U.S.A.   06

1

Benjamin J. Browning couldn't remember a birthday when he'd been more miserable. His sinuses were pounding, his eyes ached, his nose was dripping, and a hacking cough had begun to replace every third or fourth sneeze.

> *Probably the standard penance for passing thirty. Or more likely the symptom.*

The rain fell harder and his spindly red umbrella did little more than filter the downpour into a monotonous drizzle that splashed onto the crinkled brim of his rain hat and dripped in a steady stream across his abused radish of a nose.

He paused at the curb and stared vacantly into the London traffic, snarled to a standstill by the drenching rain. The city's entire taxi fleet appeared to be mired in the congestion, but there wasn't one "for-hire" light in the bunch. Browning dabbed his nose and suddenly exploded in a wrenching sneeze that completely demolished his Kleenex.

He wondered if Margaret knew how miserable he was. And how sensational this job would have to be to compensate for the cold, the rain, and no taxis. He was debating whether to stand there and wait, or try another corner, when a "for-hire" light blinked on. He hurriedly sloshed across two lanes of stalled traffic and flung himself into the taxi, only to find himself nose-to-nose with a wet, stringy-haired Afghan hound. The driver looked *back* over his shoulder.

"Sorry, guv, this one's taken."

There was no one else in the taxi except him and one smelly, bizarre-looking dog. Browning put aside his general distaste for canines.

"I'll share."

"Can't do it," the driver said. "You'll have to get out."

"I'll take seconds. You can drop the dog off first."

But the driver declined, insisting that his commission required the dog to travel alone.

Browning felt too lousy to fight, so he crawled back out into the pouring rain again, sneezed twice, then plodded off through traffic, across the square toward the West End.

Big Ben was striking the noon hour as Browning crossed through Parliament Square. He glanced up at the world's most famous clock and knew he'd never get to the office in time if he had to walk all the way. Why had Margaret done this to him? No appointment could be this important. But then, she wouldn't have called if she hadn't thought so.

Margaret was the most conscientious lady he'd ever known, and he was lucky to have her as a secretary. No, more than that. An assistant.

Browning wiped his nose, sneezed, and wiped his nose again, accomplishing very little because the Kleenex was, by now, sopping wet. He once again searched the automotive muddle before him for a taxi light and then decided to try for a bus. He stepped off the curb and headed for the bus queue on the opposite corner.

Big Ben's final toll coincided perfectly with the honk from the Morris Mini he was crossing in front of. The midget of a car pulled forward and honked again. Browning spun around, about to shout at the driver, when the car door swung open and a man beckoned to him.

Browning stared for a long moment, then stooped to look inside. The driver was all teeth, smiles, and twinkling eyes.

"Hi, sailor. Wanna ride?"

"Freddie. You're a godsend."

"I've been telling you that for years." Freddie had a sugar-coated lisp. Browning sniffed.

"Does your sunroof work?"

"Benjamin, it's raining! You must have noticed. You're all pruney."

"That's not the half of it," Browning said, tugging at the sunroof handle. "My umbrella won't fold up."

"My world. How awful."

The sunroof slid open a crack and Browning poked the umbrella handle through it. He grabbed the handle inside the car, climbed in himself, and slammed the door. "I've learned to live with it."

Freddie ground the Mini into gear and began creeping forward with the traffic. "I'll bet it's not easy. People can be so cruel."

Browning looked at him. "How would you know? Your umbrella folds up."

Browning had met Freddie on his first trip to London. They had been friends ever since. Browning had come over to investigate a racing accident for Interline, and Freddie was one of the drivers. He didn't quite fit the image of the other racing jocks and that's probably why Browning took to him. At the time, he was also having troubles trying to fit in.

When Browning graduated from college his job possibilities included being a trainee route salesman for Procter and Gamble, a computer programmer for a paper mill in Georgia, and a trainee investigator for the FBI. The last was the only job that carried any challenge with it at all, so off he went to Washington.

He lasted exactly sixteen weeks. The whole philosophy of the FBI left him cold. True, on the surface it was supposed to be an instrument of law enforcement and justice, but it was what was going on beneath the surface that he couldn't deal with. And he really didn't want to become part of it. So he left.

His next job was as a junior investigator for a large, Washington-based insurance company and in a matter of eight months he was able to parlay that into senior investigator for Knickerbocker Life in Boston.

Nine months later he was chief investigator for Interline. But the higher he got, the more paperwork, and the more time he spent behind a desk. It paid well but he didn't like it.

The trip to London one summer changed all that. He fell in love with the city, and with Paris and Amsterdam, where he had to fly to interview drivers involved in the accident. And with Nice and Madrid, where he went on his second trip to investigate the food poisoning of a planeload of tourists from Milwaukee.

All in all, Browning and the investigators under him made seventeen trips to Europe in less than a year. So Browning saw his way out of company politics and mounting paperwork by resigning from the company, moving to London, and making a deal with Interline to investigate all their European claims on a guaranteed first-serve, free-lance basis. It would also give him a chance to get into more challenging areas of investigation.

Browning blinked. He didn't believe his eyes. Freddie was driving his baby-wheeled toy car right down the middle of a sidewalk, scattering wet pedestrians with his horn. Traffic in the street was at a complete standstill, and Freddie's impatience had finally gotten the best of him.

At the intersection, the car bounced off the curb, dribbling Browning's head against the ceiling like a basketball; then it turned left and raced down the wrong side of the street for half a block, finally turning right into a narrow alley.

"There's something terribly macho about driving fast, don't you think?" giggled Freddie.

"No, Freddie, I don't," squeaked Browning.

2

The Morris Mini with the optional red umbrella jolted to a stop by the curb next to a *no-entry*, one-way street. "Are you sure?" Freddie asked. "It wouldn't take a minute to spin around the block and take you right to the door."

Browning grappled for the door handle, yanked it open, and leaped to the safety of solid ground. Then he turned to extract the umbrella handle from the sunroof and peered down at Freddie through the hole.

"Freddie, out there somewhere the Angel of Death has just been cheated and I don't imagine he's happy about it so I'm not about to give him another shot."

"Really, Benjamin. It's not like you were driving with an amateur. I'm a professional racer, for Pete's sake."

Browning squatted and looked through the window at Freddie. "I've got a great idea," he said. "Let's go into business together selling off shares of your life insurance policy."

Freddie slammed the door and ground the gearshift into first. "Good-bye, Benjamin."

Browning stood up. "See ya later, Freddie."

And, as he turned from the car, his day's luck continued in form. He was immediately flattened by a supersonic young lady, racing to catch a bus. The impact launched Browning's red umbrella into orbit and catapulted the lady's package from Harrod's into a mid-street trajectory. Browning bounced off Freddie's car and managed to intercept the package, but the lady shopper, with nothing to bounce upon, landed in a heap atop the little red umbrella, trashing it completely.

Freddie looked out the car window. "Is anyone hurt?"

Browning didn't hear him. He was gazing through the pouring rain at what must surely be one of the world's most beautiful women. Even sprawled on the sidewalk, soaking wet, she was breathtaking.

From a hollow distance somewhere, Browning thought he heard Freddie say, "I guess not." And the little roller skate of a car sped off.

"I'm sorry," said Breathtaking, blinking away the raindrops from her long, natural lashes.

Browning sniffed, totally entranced. "It's all my fault."

8

The fall had separated her rain hat from her long brown hair, which was soaked, and clinging, and beautiful. Browning's stomach was doing flip-flops and somewhere an eighty-piece orchestra was playing the theme from *Love Story*. He wondered if she heard it and wondered if he should ask her.

"No. I was running entirely too fast," said Breathtaking.

Browning sniffed. She probably didn't hear the orchestra. "I shouldn't have stepped in your way without looking," he heard himself say. But he knew that wasn't really him, for he was running toward her in slow motion through a field of yellow daisies.

"Was this your umbrella?" she said, glancing down at the mangled umbrella beneath her.

Now there was a chorus. Fifty voices. And she was running in slow motion toward *him*. "It's okay. I won't need it when the rain stops."

A little smile crinkled across her face, and Browning gasped for breath, feeling that he was going to totally explode any moment. She felt it too, he thought. Why else would she be running toward him in slow motion through a field of daisies?

"Would you mind helping me up?" she said.

Browning wondered why he hadn't thought of that. He reached for her hand. "I'm sorry . . . I . . . I mean, you are just so . . ."

They bumped slightly as he pulled her up,

and their eyes met in a long moment of tingling silence. Browning swallowed, sniffed, and relinquished possession of her package from Harrod's.

"Thank you for saving this," said Breathtaking. "It's a crystal wine decanter."

She was indebted to him. Things couldn't be working out better.

"It's the least I can do after dumping you in a puddle like that."

"You're an American," she said in her perfect London accent.

They shared a silly grin as the rain began to come down harder. Finally, Breathtaking took a step backward.

"Well, thanks for everything." And she turned to leave.

"Wait! Uhh . . . if you're not doing anything tonight. . . ."

Breathtaking turned back and once again their eyes met with a tingle. This is it, thought Browning. He reached for her in slow motion, and she for him. The smell of daisies was everywhere and the music was at crescendo, all eighty pieces and fifty voices playing and singing at the same time. They drew closer, and finally they touched.

"I'm sorry. I'll be in Paris."

Figures. She hadn't heard the orchestra, or the chorus, or anything. If she had, Paris could wait. She probably didn't like him at all. What a fool he had made of himself!

"Maybe . . . uhh . . . when you get back?" Browning sniffed.

She stared at him for a long moment, the rain splashing against her cheeks, and the music started again. Why was she torturing him like this? Just say "no" and go on.

"Why not? My name's Jackie. I write for *Time*-Europe. Call me on Friday."

Enter the chorus. The music swells.

"Can't Friday. How about Monday?" Browning heard himself say.

"Okay." And she disappeared into the rain and the crowds.

Long after she was gone, Browning was still standing and staring after her. Finally, he lifted the crumpled umbrella over his head and trudged up the one-way street, dissolving himself into a sea of bobbing black umbrellas.

Browning's office was in a small, older building on a narrow street in the Soho district. He felt Soho was London at its best. Total variety. People from all over the world, all walks of life, all professions, all types. Within any given block. It helped keep life interesting to have an office there. But he wouldn't want to live there.

Browning shared a building with the London office of the William Morris Agency, one of the world's largest talent agencies. They were on *two* and he was on *three*, and he claimed to have a phobia about small elevators because he liked to walk up the stairs and pass the William Morris reception room, just to see who was there.

Last week he had seen Jill Clayburgh sitting

on the reception couch, reading a magazine just like a normal person. And a month ago he had bumped into Sally Field stepping off the elevator, and it nearly sent him into cardiac arrest. He had been in love with her since the first episode of *The Flying Nun*, and for weeks after the elevator episode, he spent several hours a day wishing he were Burt Reynolds.

Today there was no one interesting in the William Morris reception room, so he waved at Penny and trudged on up the stairs, dragging his ruptured parasol behind him. He sniffed and sneezed and felt miserable, but through it all, there was a warm glow conjured by the image of Jackie's face looking at him through the pouring rain.

At the top of the stairs, he turned left and sloshed down the narrow hallway to a door that advertised the home of Browning and Shackleton — Private Investigators. He paused for a moment, preparing himself for Margaret's nannylike fussing, and then he went in.

"Oh, Mr. Browning, just look at you. You're wet from head to toe. You'll surely catch pneumonia."

"Margaret, I already have pneumonia. Tell me about the phone call."

Margaret was already on him, checking his forehead and unbuttoning his raincoat to see if his clothes were wet. Browning put up with her mothering because she was probably the best thing that had ever happened to him. Sometimes he couldn't help but feel guilty, however, because though it had never been mentioned, he was certain that Margaret was in love with him. He was right, of course, but through the three years and seven months that Margaret had been with Benjamin Browning, she had managed to transfer all such feelings into terms of motherly love, satisfying her need for outward expression in the form of parental concern. This, even though she was only seven years older than he. But it seemed to work. At least on the surface.

"If it hadn't sounded terribly important you know I wouldn't have called," Margaret was saying.

"I know."

"He insisted that he see you today but he wouldn't say why. I tried desperately to find out because you don't need to be out in this weather over a trifle. But he wouldn't even tell me his name. Only that the meeting was important and terribly urgent."

"It's okay, Margaret. You did your best. Now, why don't you go on to lunch. Here."

He handed her the remnants of the red umbrella and for a long moment Margaret just stared at the twisted ruins.

"Do you want to have it recovered again?"

"No. I think it's over. Better take it out and shoot it. And give it a proper burial."

Margaret left the room holding the umbrella out by her fingertips as if it were a dead rat. Browning turned, dragged himself into his inner office, and plopped down behind his desk, dripping hat, sopping raincoat, and all.

He dug into his pocket, withdrew a bottle of cough medicine, and took a long swig . . . of nothing. It was empty.

"Crud!"

His throat hurt, his sinuses were pounding, and then he remembered the bottle. He reached for a nearby cigar box, delicately removed a false bottom, and retrieved a small bottle of Metaxa, remnant of his first trip to Athens to investigate a claim against Coca-Cola.

He took a long swig. It brought pleasant relief. As an afterthought, he filled the medicine bottle and then glanced at his watch. His appointment was late.

"If that guy doesn't show, I'll kill him," he said aloud.

It was a safe thing to say, of course, because if he didn't show, Browning wouldn't know who he was. He lit a cigar, withdrew the thermometer from his coat pocket, stuffed both into his mouth, and turned to scowl out the window. After a moment, his thoughts were interrupted by a man's voice.

"Benjamin Browning?"

Browning turned to see a dark, stony-faced man of about forty-five. His expensive black topcoat, thin, jet-black hair, and cold, penetrating eyes made Browning wonder if the angel of death had come to put him out of his misery.

"My name is Quimby Charles. I spoke with your secretary."

Browning stood, took the cigar out of his mouth, but forgot the thermometer.

"Ymrf. Mrffl." Browning was gesturing toward a chair. He removed the thermometer and tried again. "Have a seat."

Browning sat down, trying to read the thermometer. "I'm trying to shake a rather nasty cold, and don't seem to be doing a very good job of it." He looked up at Charles, who had chosen to remain standing. "What can I do for you?"

"I want to buy protection for someone."

"I see."

Browning withdrew the medicine bottle from his pocket, took a swig, and offered one to Charles. The tall, dark man declined with a touch of disdain that Browning tried to ignore as he dropped the bottle into the top desk drawer. He began to doodle Charles's name on the desk pad.

"I'm not in the protection business," he finally said. "I'm an investigator. Perhaps I could recommend a security service."

"I want you, Mr. Browning, because I know you'll do it right . . . and I know you'll be discreet."

"You know my work?"

"I know your work *permit*. It would be a shame if it were not renewed just when you were beginning to do so well."

And the man placed a large stack of money onto the desk in front of Browning. At least two inches thick, and the top bill was a one-hundred pound note. Browning gazed at the windfall.

"You in organized crime?"

"I'm in Parliament."

Browning shrugged. "Six of one . . ."

The man withdrew a neatly folded slip of paper from his pocket and handed it to Browning.

"This is her name and address. I have reason to believe she is in extreme danger and I'd like you to start immediately."

Browning took the paper and studied it.

"A her, huh?"

"No questions, Mr. Browning. Just protection. The threat should be over in a few days, a week at the most. I'll contact you."

Browning glanced at the stack of money, looked at the rain-drenched street, then turned to Charles.

"Can I borrow your umbrella?"

3

The rain continued. Hard rain. Heavy and consistent. Much more of this, thought Browning, and London will be floating. He remembered the first time he saw London flood, and what a surprise it was. London and rain were supposed to go together. At least that had always been his impression and he couldn't even remember why.

He paid the taxi driver, pulled his collar up, and withdrew into it like a turtle, then splashed across the street to the Carlton Arms Apartments. The doorman opened the door from the inside, apparently having had his fill of the weather, and Browning was surprised to find that he was expected. He was given Patricia Elliot's flat number and directed toward the elevator with a smile.

Upstairs he stood dripping on a Persian white

carpet for an eternity, waiting for someone to open the door to Flat 3A. But no one did. He rang the bell for the third time and checked his watch. But there was still no response. Finally he banged on the door, only once, because the first knock found it unlatched and it swung open.

For a long moment Browning just stared into the dark room, wondering how he'd ever gotten into this business when he was so easily frightened. He nudged the door open another inch or two.

"Miss Elliot??" He stretched for a peak into the room. "Miss Elliott???"

The light from the doorway sprinkled across a very expensively furnished room. A silk brocade loveseat, a Monsoir crystal lamp, an original Jean Pierre Arnaud, and a number of exquisite sculptures. Miss Elliot was definitely a lover of art.

Browning took a single step inside, hesitated, then stepped deeper into the room, turning as he went to look full circle. Then suddenly he froze. He had backed into something. Something pointed, sticking into the back of his neck.

"Miss Elliot?" he said meekly.

There was no response.

Slowly he turned and came nose-to-nose with a stainless steel sculpture of a man. A definite prizewinner in the category of "Most Bizarre."

He looked away, and a thin wafer of light slicing under a door on the far side of the room caught his eye.

"Miss Elliot?"

No response. He forced himself across the darkened room, paused at the door and listened for a moment, then pushed through, hoping desperately to find his charge on the other side.

He did. But he wished he hadn't. Patricia Elliot lay on the kitchen floor in a pool of blood streaming from a stab wound in her back.

Browning shivered, then spun to face the darkness through the doorway. He had heard something. Or thought he had. Silently he listened, then finally turned back to the body and kneeled to perform the obligatory but unnecessary pulse check. This time he *did* hear something but he spun too late. A gleaming flash, a gloved hand, a sudden blaze of pain, then nothing. Browning's lifeless body dropped across Patricia Elliot's. The gloved hand snatched a delicate gold pendant from the dead woman's neck . . . and then the room was still.

4

He remembered the pain, and the colors, lots of them. Then black. Everything black. But only for a moment. The infusion of a bright light, building in intensity until there was nothing left but pure white.

Then there was a voice. A man's voice, with a thick, New England accent. Like the man who did those clam chowder commercials.

"Welcome to IDEF, young fella. And before you say it, there's been no mistake. Accordin' to your file here, that was definitely your NTT."

Browning could see him now. It was happening like a fade-in in a movie. Slowly the image took shape. He saw a little old man who looked to be about sixty. He was sitting behind a white metal desk in a very small cubicle of an office that reminded Browning of the room back in Boston, where he once spent seven hours having his tax return audited. Only this one was mostly all-white, the decor a strange concoction of bureaucratic plain, yesterday and tomorrow. Two walls were almost completely glass-paneled, but through the glass there was nothing but white, fluffy, lazily wafting clouds — or somebody with a big dry-ice machine.

Browning himself was sitting in a rickety, wooden swivel chair, across the desk from the little man and directly beneath a large, translucent cylinder that looked to Browning as if it were about to swallow him.

There were rows and rows of file cabinets, covering one complete wall, all made out of some sort of cloudy material. And there were several long tubes, like the pneumatic tubes that used to run through department stores back in the 1940s to whisk messages or money in little metal cartridges from one department to another. Only *these* tubes were made of transparent material, and the cartridges whizzing through them were of many different colors. Two of the tubes emptied into a basket on the man's desk.

There was something else weird about the room, but Browning couldn't put his finger on it. He glanced down at himself. He was wearing a white hospital gown. No wonder his seat felt cold.

"What's an NTT?" queried Browning.

The man was punching keys on a white computer.

"Natural Termination Time."

The computer spit out a piece of paper.

"You mean this is not a hospital?"

The man tore the piece of paper from the machine and turned to face Browning, thrusting the paper in front of him.

"If you'll just sign here."

Browning was beginning to hope desperately that he would wake up and find himself at home in bed. He scratched his name across the paper.

"What am I signing?"

"You're acknowledging that you are dead and you agree to all the terms and conditions thereof."

"I was afraid it was something like that. I don't *feel* dead."

The man reached for the paper. "A mere technicality, Mr. Browning. You are definitely D-A-D." And he pounded a rubber stamp down onto the signed paper.

"D-A-D?" questioned Browning.

"Dead as a Doornail," said the man. "This paper makes it official." He dropped the paper into a large file tray labeled *MM*.

"Unfortunately, you are also **MM. Marginal Material.**"

The man turned to the computer and typed something into it. "Seems like that's all we get anymore."

A chart, which looked to Browning like the corporate structure for AT&T, appeared on the computer screen and the man flipped a switch that transferred it to a big screen behind his desk.

"In my day you had your *good* and you had your *bad*. But not today. Haven't seen a saint since the sixteenth century, and the last clear-cut candidate for eternal damnation was just after World War II." He turned to Browning and shook his head. "I guess everybody quit trying."

Browning was beginning to fear the worst. This was all happening for real. A red cartridge raced through one of the clear tubes, chased by a green cartridge.

"Anyway. My name is Mr. Higgins and I'm your counselor." Higgins picked up the rubber stamp he had used earlier, twisted the handle, and a laser beam approximately four feet in length sprung from it. Browning felt himself recoil a bit and Higgins smiled.

"We had it before *Star Wars*."

He turned to the large computer screen and, using the laser, pointed to the letters IDEF in the center of the chart.

"You are currently at the Intermediate Destination Evaluation Facility, where it will be determined whether or not you will go up to your Ultimate Reward" — He pointed to UR on the chart — "or down to Eternal Damnation." The laser pointed to ED. Higgins turned back to Browning, retracted the laser into the handle of the rubber stamp, and produced a file folder labeled FAA.

"To help us make this determination you will be given a Final Assessment Assignment before moving on, and that means you have to go back."

The words aroused Browning's adrenaline, or whatever it was they used up here.

"Go back???"

Higgins opened the file. "Your Final Assessment Assignment is to go back and solve your own murder."

Browning wondered if he heard wrong. Either that, or his luck must be changing.

"Solve my own murder?"

"This is not a wedding ceremony, Mr. Browning. You are not obligated to repeat everything I say."

But Browning wasn't listening. He could see himself at the bank, making a deposit.

"The book royalties alone will be worth a fortune. I mean, how many people get to go back to Earth after they're dead?" He was talking more to himself than to Higgins, but the answer came from across the desk.

"Oh, two, maybe three hundred a day. And writing a book will be quite impossible."

Higgins was peering at him over his glasses and even *looked* like the little old man who did the clam chowder commercials. Browning was tempted to ask him if he was.

"How come?"

"Trust me, Mr. Browning."

The slightest of smiles tugged at Higgins' otherwise flat expression, and Browning suspected he was better off not knowing exactly what he meant.

*Stop it. This is absurd. I refuse to believe
that this is really happening. Wake up!*

"Apparently an innocent man has been charged
with your murder as well as with the murder of
a Miss Patricia Elliot. His name is Quimby
Charles." Higgins was looking at the front page
of a London *Daily Mirror*.

Quimby Charles. The name echoed in Browning's head, repeating itself. *Quimby Charles. Was
it yesterday, or today?* It seemed like years ago,
or never. He knew it was there but he couldn't
find it. *Who is Quimby Charles?!* Then it hit him.

"That's the man who hired me!"

And he reached for the newspaper and looked
at the front page. "That's *not* the man who hired
me."

At the bottom of the page was a large picture
of a distinguished man probably in his sixties. The
cutline read: "Quimby Charles: Member of Parliament, Elliot Fiance." But it definitely wasn't the
man who had come to Browning's office.

At the top of the page, above the photograph
of Patricia Elliot, a banner headline screamed:
"SOCIALITE AND LOVER KILLED, FIANCE
CHARGED."

"*Socialite and lover?*" He looked at Higgins.
"That lousy creep set me up!"

"Please watch your language, Mr. Browning.
Remember where you are."

Higgins was signing a pink form, in triplicate.

He tore off the top copy, stuffed it into a red cartridge, and fed it to the transparent tube. It was sucked away into the clouds outside Higgins' office. He tore off the second copy and handed it to Browning.

"Take this down to RRDD, the second door on the left down the hall."

"What's it for?"

"It's a Returnable Requisition Order. You certainly can't go back in your own body."

"Why not?"

Higgins sighed. "It has a hole in it."

"Oh." And Browning was suddenly obsessed with the urge to reach back and stick his finger in the hole. Instead, he pulled himself out of the chair and started for the door.

The door . . . the door . . .

Now he knew. He was absolutely certain. This was definitely a dream and the dreammaker had screwed up. There was no door in the office. None. Zero. Four walls. Those weird translucent file cabinets. The big picture windows with the clouds. But no doors.

"Please sit down, Mr. Browning."

"Oh, buzz off!" said Browning. "I'm sick of this dream."

"I've asked you to watch your language, Mr. Browning. You may consider this a warning. Now please sit down."

*When am I gonna wake up? What if it's
not a dream?*

"Mr. Browning, if you do not follow instructions, I shall be forced to revoke your FAA and
send you directly down to ED."

It wasn't worth the risk. Browning sat down.
The large translucent cylinder above him
slowly descended until it completely covered him
and he could no longer see Mr. Higgins. Then,
suddenly, he felt his stomach flip, like with the
drop of a fast elevator. And that was all.

5

The Returnable Requisition Dispersal Department reminded Browning of a giant welfare office, only it too was all-white and cloudy. Except for the small colorful cartridges that whished overhead through a maze of clear tubing. And the colored lines on the floor leading to the long counter that ran the length of the room. It was a mixture of early civil service and science fiction.

Hundreds of people — all dressed like Browning in short, white hospital gowns, all barefooted and all wearing small brass discs, like dog tags, around their necks — stood in long, impersonal lines, each leading to a bored, impersonal clerk behind the counter.

Browning had expected to still be in Higgins' office when his transport cylinder lifted, and he was first surprised, then distressed, at what he saw. Masses. Numbers. It looked like the military. Back home, he could have understood being just a number, but not here! Not in Heaven! It was against everything he'd been taught by the movies.

He was ordered into the red line, and immediately tried to strike up a conversation with the pretty blonde ahead of him, but she didn't want to talk much. She was still angry because she had spent three years working on some guy, finally got him to propose, and the same afternoon was hit by a Greyhound bus. An elderly lady in the light green line next to Browning wanted to talk, but only about how badly they had treated her at the rest home.

When it was his turn at the counter, he presented his Returnable Requisition Order to a large, imposing German woman with gray hair knotted in a tight bun, possibly accounting for her mean disposition.

She barked at Browning without looking up from her work.

"Computer Identification Number!"

"Pardon?"

She looked at him with a withering glare. "I said Computer Identification Number."

"I'm sorry . . . I . . . uhh . . . didn't know I had one."

That was obviously the wrong answer because she grabbed the brass disc around his neck and yanked it across the counter, practically strangling him in the process. Reading from the disc, she copied down the number: "BJB-779."

She heaved open a huge ledger, swirling nearby papers into the air. Browning straightened his gown and waited patiently as she went down a long list. Finally: "Seven months. Maybe six if you're not picky about sex." She slammed the book shut. "Next!"

Browning never ceased to be amazed at how bureaucracy could confound even the simplest of communications.

"I'm afraid you don't understand. You see, I have to go back *now*. Today. This minute."

The clerk looked again at the Requisition Order and found Browning to be right, a fact that didn't make her any happier.

"Why can't they write so someone could read it?"

She slammed the big book shut, shoved it aside, and tackled another one equally as large. Browning had seen mean before. And ugly. But never in such perfect combination.

"An immediate return means you take an LGR."

Browning didn't like the sound of it but he asked anyway.

"An LGR?"

The clerk looked up and there was a twinkle of sadistic pleasure in her eye. "Lower Grade Returnable."

She looked back to the book.

"Anthropoid, bovine, equine, rodent, marsupial, pachyderm, crustacean, canine . . ."

Whoa! Hold everything! She's talking about animals! Browning hit the ceiling.

"Wait a minute! I'm not going back as an animal! I want a person. I have an assignment. I have to solve a murder. Get an innocent man out of jail, for Pete's sake! How can I do that as an animal?"

"For immediate return, I have a dog, small, mongrel. Due to be hit by a garbage truck in forty-five seconds."

"I wanna see Mr. Higgins!" Browning screeched. "He didn't say anything about animals!"

The hulk of a clerk handed him his Requisition Order, and smiled. "Mr. Higgins suggested you return as a rat."

Browning looked at the paper and his stomach knotted tight. He remembered Higgins' little smile.

"I'll kill him!" he bellowed.

Poof! The intimidating German clerk suddenly melted into a soft-spoken quiver.

"Oh, I just love the way you say that."

The clerk was reaching for him.

"You come with me and we'll make sure you don't go back to Earth as some old rat."

The last thing Browning wanted to do was go with her. She took his hand, lifted the countertop, and led him, rather, pulled him toward her. Browning looked up at her and suddenly a dog, small, mongrel, sounded sensational.

"What about the garbage truck? You know, the dog?"

The clerk was dripping sugar now. "I'm sure there will be another along soon. Are you really in that much of a hurry?"

"Oh, yes. A big hurry. A very big hurry. Terribly important. Right now. Garbage truck. For sure."

She wrinkled her nose and blinked at him, a sight few people in the world deserved to see. "Well, all right. But I'll be waiting for you when you get back."

Browning had trouble even forcing a weak smile. "Right."

She pushed him down into a chair, wiggled her tongue at him, and stood back as the large translucent tube consumed him. He saw her reach for the red button and suddenly the squealing sound of screeching tires and blaring horns was deafening.

That was close!!

Those were his first thoughts as a dog. A small, cute, fluffy dog that had just come within a few inches of being hit by a garbage truck. A huge, large, giant of a garbage truck.

Browning was cowering in the doorway of a women's boutique, still shaking from the experience. He looked up at the steady rush of bustling pedestrians. Way up.

> *I never realized how big everything looks from down here.*

He glanced back at himself, trying to get some perspective on what he looked like. He sniffed one of his feet, then checked his tail.

I feel so naked.

He wished desperately that he could still believe he was dreaming. That was the only logical way to deal with this. And, whatever else he was, Browning was a logical person. Or had been. Now he was a logical dog. Which, of course, wasn't logical at all.

He sneezed.

Terrific. They left me the cold.

He shook himself, which, frankly, felt incredibly good, then looked up and down the street.

When I was a man, I spoke and acted like a man. But now it is time to put away my manish ways and act like a dog.

He shook himself again and looked Heavenward.

You people up there are sick, you know that?

The best place for him to start, he decided, was the scene of the crime. So he set out on his four spindly legs and walked toward the corner, hoping to get some idea of how far he was from Patricia Elliot's apartment.

Apparently quite a way, because as he turned the corner, there before him thrusting majestically into the sky, was Paris' Eiffel Tower.

Paris, he groaned, and looked Heavenward.

How am I going to get to London?

34

A car door slammed and Browning looked. It was a red convertible, top down, with British right-hand drive. A portly gentleman in his late fifties was standing in the street talking to the lady driver. Actually, portly was an understatement and Browning wondered how he had fit into the car in the first place. And once in, how he had gotten out. But, of course, that wasn't important. The important thing was he was speaking with a British accent.

"I'll call you tonight. Will you be in London or the country house?"

The lady's back was to Browning but he heard her answer clearly. "London."

He looked back to the sky.

Sorry. How was I to know?

And he moved cautiously toward the rear of the car.

"You have my new number?" the lady was asking.

"Yes. And please remember, Jacquelyn, make it sexy or it won't sell ten copies."

"You just get the contract drawn. We'll talk about sexy later."

"Don't tease me, Jackie. You know how I feel about you."

"Like a father."

"I'll try to remember that."

Browning was on the other side of the car gauging the jump. He, of course, had no idea if his new legs were good jumpers or not. But he

35

did know he was going to London, one way or another.

"Bernie, I appreciate the opportunity. I really do."

"Just write a good book. I'll talk to you tonight."

Browning was in the seat next to her when she turned away from Bernie. Their eyes met and the impact nearly sent Browning into cardiac arrest, for there, not three feet from his wet little nose, was *her*. Her from the rain. The wet lady from *Time* magazine. She blinked.

"Do I know you?"

His heart was pounding, his gaze froze. He probably couldn't have answered if he were human. She was lovely. She was gorgeous. And here he was with four legs and a tail.

Jackie Howard had been with *Time* magazine for almost two years, and before that, six years with the *Evening Standard*. First she wrote obituaries, then gardening, then finally the hard stuff. Politics.

She had handled an interview for the regular political reporter of the *Standard* — an important interview with the Prime Minister. Under his name, of course.

It happened quite by accident and completely without her editor's knowledge or approval. She had been eating her usual lunch, a hamburger at the Great American Disaster, when the call came. Jason Hemmings had a two o'clock interview with the Prime Minister. Unfortunately Jason was in Paris. It seems his pre-marriage bachelor party had been held the night before and his friends, in the spirit of celebration, had put him on a plane to Paris. He hadn't realized until it was too late.

Jackie didn't question the story. If it was a lie, Jason's imagination deserved the credit of belief. And besides, he was asking her to cover for him. Her. Jackie Howard. She was going to interview the Prime Minister. And write an important story.

The only problem was that everybody loved it. The readers, the editor, the publisher, even the Prime Minister. So Jason had taken the editor out, bought him several drinks, and finally, when he thought the time was right, told him that Jackie had written the story.

From there it was only a short distance to the front page, and a year later on to *Time* magazine. And throughout that year and the next two, Bernie had been promising to find just the right topic for her first book. And at last he had come through. But it wasn't the book causing her current worry. It was a dog. And she really felt weird just staring at him wondering why she was feeling so weird. It felt like she'd been here before, but not really. It felt dumb.

The eyes. It must be the eyes. They were incredible.

But there was still something more. The eyes were hypnotic, but there was still something more.

You're cracking up, Jackie. You're going over the edge. The news about the book must have been too much.

She blinked and shook it off. "I hate to disappoint you but I'm afraid you'll have to get out. I'm leaving immediately for England and I'm quite sure you don't want to go there."

Browning promptly lay down on the seat and closed both eyes.

7

The London traffic was jammed as usual. And Jackie was still like an iceberg. She had both hands on the steering wheel and Browning was balancing his chin in the crook of her arm, looking up at her with as much pleading as his big brown eyes could muster. The traffic light had been red for almost thirty seconds when she finally glanced down at him.

"Don't come making up to me. I don't like dogs who bite."

I didn't bite, I growled. And what choice did I have? You tried to throw me out.

Jackie continued to gaze down at him until her smirk finally melted into surrender. She sighed. "What am I going to do with you?"

She reached down and gently scratched his ear.

Not that, or I'm going to be in deep trouble.

Her touch seemed to drain away all intelligence from Browning's head; he began to sway in slow rhythm to her scratching.

"You can't be a watchdog. You're too cute and fluffy to be dangerous."

Don't count on it.

She toyed with the brass tag dangling from Browning's collar. "What does BJB-779 mean?"

It's my initials and my computer ID number.

"Do you mind if I just call you BJ for short?"

Don't say short. I'm sensitive about my height.

A blast from a horn brought Jackie's eyes back to the light. It was green. She drove three blocks and turned right on Beauchamp Place. Browning perked up.

This is perfect. You're headed right where I need to go. Just take a left at the next street . . .

But Jackie took a right.

No problem. Take a left right here and we'll still be okay.

But Jackie took another right.

*Okay, that's it. I can see that we're going
to have to go our separate ways. Not that
I want to, mind you, I mean we've
hardly given it a fair chance. But I've got
this job to do, and anyway, what can it
all come to? Another time, another place
... but let's face it. I'm a dog and you're
a person. Granted one of the most
wonderful persons I've ever known, but
I mean really, what can it come to?*

Jackie turned left.

*You don't happen to know any cute little
poodles, do you?*

The car whipped into the entry drive of the
Brockton Apartments and the doorman had
Jackie's door open before it reached a full stop.

"Miss Howard. Did you have a nice trip? How
was Paris?"

"Warm for this time of year, actually," said
Jackie, climbing out of the car. "Otherwise super.
Would you get my suitcase in the trunk and I'll
get the dog." She turned to retrieve Browning,
but the seat was empty. Browning was halfway
down the block.

"BJ?"

He stopped and looked back over his shoulder.

*Please. This is hard enough without
tears.*

The red double-decker bus lumbered to a stop.
Browning was standing in line as if it were an

everyday occurrence and, in his turn, climbed aboard. As the bus pulled away he thought he was home free when suddenly it stopped and he felt two large hands surround his rib cage. He landed abruptly in the middle of the street.

Racist.

He watched the bus drive off, then gave himself a good shake — again reveling in how good it felt — and trotted off down the street.

Browning rounded the corner, but he was no longer trotting. Trudging would be a better word. And panting. It was easy to see that his *returnable* had not been a lover of exercise. What's more, the pads on his feet hurt.

He stopped and looked up at the Carlton Arms, Patricia Elliot's ex-home. It looked the same as it did before, only a little taller. And the front door was open. Browning wondered if it was guarded.

One way to find out.

He gathered himself up, trotted across the street, and pranced right through the door.

Hi. Maybe you remember me. I got killed here.

They didn't. He came sailing back through the door and landed in a heap.

Two for two. So much for the direct approach.

He trotted around to an alley where he found a fire escape zigzagging up the side of the building.

A definitely possibility if the trash cans below were tall enough for him to reach the bottom step. He studied the windows above for a moment, then started for the trash cans.

Wait a minute. What was that?

Something moved. A tail. A long, yellow, fluffy tail curling out of one of the cans. It disappeared, then reappeared, attached to . . . a cat.

A chill shot down Browning's back and his hair stood on end. He didn't understand. He liked cats, or used to. He heard himself issue a nasty, but involuntary, bark. The cat spun into a coiled crouch, then quite suddenly relaxed, and Browning heard a voice, a high tenor voice with a lisp.

Oh, it's you. Higgins said you were coming.

Browning jerked around to look behind him, then both ways down the alley, then back to the cat.

It's me, dummy. Kitty, Kitty. I'm a returnable too.

Browning spotted the little brass disc hanging around the cat's neck.

You mean I can hear you think?

The Lord works in mysterious ways, but then doesn't everybody up there?

The voice had an unmistakably familiar ring. More than familiar. The fact was there was only one voice like that in the entire world.

Freddie??!

I'm afraid so.

Browning was stunned. Seeing himself as a dog was one thing, but seeing Freddie as a cat was more than his equilibrium could handle. He stepped closer to the trash cans.

What happened?

Oh, about six blocks from where I let you out the other day I took a shortcut through this one-lane alley and . . . well . . . I'd've never guessed a truck that big could get into an alley that small. My car looked like a bottle cap. They had to take me to the returnable desk in a baggie.

I wonder if dogs can cry.

That's very sweet, Benjamin. But it's not really necessary.

Not for you. For how much I could have made off your life insurance.

Don't be tacky. It doesn't become you.

Freddie jumped down and circled Browning a couple of times.

*Patricia Elliot's kitchen window is the
one with the porcelain albatross on the
sill. The window latch is broken so
there's no problem getting in. I went up
to steal some food from her refrigerator
this morning but everything's rotted
since she died.*

As he made his last round, Freddie's tail
brushed BJ's and Browning danced sideways.

Cut that out!

*Well, I've gotta run. Maybe I'll see you
later.*

He paused nose-to-nose with Browning.

I just love your big brown eyes.

Browning took a step backward, marveling at
how much the cat actually looked like Freddie.

Good-bye, Freddie.

Freddie turned and trotted off down the alley,
glancing back over his shoulder.

*If you see Higgins tell him never mind
about sending the rats. I tried one and
don't like them.*

At the sound of the crash, the shadowy figure spun around from the open desk drawer. It was the phony Quimby Charles. He quickly shut the drawer and silently disappeared into a closet, quietly closing the door behind him.

Browning crouched frozen on the window sill, listening for sounds of life. The remains of the white porcelain albatross were scattered on the floor below. Looks better, Browning thought. Then, hearing nothing, he jumped to the floor and walked through the kitchen, carefully avoiding, but pausing to look at, the taped outlines of his and Patricia's bodies on the floor. It felt strange being in the room where he had been killed.

At the kitchen door, he listened for a moment then pushed through into the living room. It was just as he remembered it. Bizarre. Especially the stainless steel statue.

Up three steps and to the right was sort of a studio. It was a disarray of drawings, sketches, photographs of art objects, swatches of cloth, and magazines. He started with the desk. One at a time he nudged open the drawers and pawed through the contents, wishing he had some idea of what he was looking for.

Across the room a closet door silently cracked open. Inside, cloaked in the shadows, was the dark man who had posed as Quimby Charles. He watched Browning methodically dig through the desk drawers. The man cracked the door wider to see if anyone else was in the room, but the phony Mr. Charles saw nothing or no one except a fluffy brown dog, now on top of the desk, and pawing through a stack of photographs.

Browning was looking for pictures of people, but there weren't any. They were all pictures of rooms in various stages of decoration. Before and after photographs.

He turned his attention to the desk calendar. It was opened to September 16th.

Hmm. She was killed on the 15th so why is this turned to the 16th?

He flipped over a page with his paw and got his answer. There *was* no 15th. That page was missing.

Inside the closet, the cold and penetrating eyes of the dark man glanced down to his long muscular fingers now unfolding the missing calendar page. The name Malcolm Bart was written opposite three o'clock, artistically lettered in red with a felt-tip pen. He looked back at Browning and his mouth fell open in disbelief.

The small dog had a pencil in his mouth, shading a calendar page, trying to outline the impression of what might have been written on the page above. Unfortunately it didn't work. His efforts showed nothing.

Curse the guy who invented felt-tip pens.

He flipped back to the fourteenth. There was a phone number on the page, written elegantly in red. He decided to try it, just to see who answered. He needed a lead. Something. Anything! He lifted the phone off the hook.

The man in the closet stared in shock at a dog making a telephone call. He eased the door open a little wider.

After struggling with the first two numbers, Browning finally decided his furry paw was too large and cumbersome a tool to deal with the dialing apparatus of the telephone. So he resorted to the old "pencil-in-the-mouth" trick to dial the number. A man answered.

"Needham Gallery."

Never heard of it.

The voice on the phone repeated itself.

"Needham Gallery!"

Browning cocked a mischievous look at the phone . . . then barked.

"Pardon?"

Browning hung up the phone.

> *Well, it's a start. I wonder where this*
> *Needham Gallery is.*

He glanced around the room, looking for a phone book.

> *Wait a minute.*

The closet door was open. And he could have sworn it hadn't been before.

Click, click.

The front door was being unlocked. Then a man's voice: ". . . and I don't think I should be doing this."

Browning glanced around, looking for a hiding place. Was he seeing things or did that closet door across the room suddenly close itself? The voices got closer and Browning finally dove under the desk for refuge.

He pulled himself into a tight ball in the darkest corner and listened. It was a man and a woman, now in the same room. And the woman's voice sounded familiar. Very familiar. He stretched for a peek and came face-to-face with . . . Jackie.

"BJ?? What are you doing here?"

She picked him up and put him on the desk, totally bewildered by his presence. The man freaked.

"Oh, my. I had no idea she had a dog. All animals are supposed to be registered with the office. Scotland Yard will think I was withholding something. Oh, my . . ."

Jackie was only half listening. She had never been superstitious, but this was stretching the limits of statistical probability. And she was having that strange feeling again.

"I don't think so."

"I beg your pardon?"

"I don't think he belonged to Patricia Elliot," Jackie said.

"He's here! In a locked flat! How could you conclude otherwise?"

"He was in Paris this morning."

"Surely you are mistaken. How could a dog get from Paris to London?"

"I brought him."

"Oh, then he's *your* dog."

"No, he isn't."

"Then he must be Miss Elliot's."

"I don't think so."

Browning felt like a spectator at a tennis match, looking back and forth from one to the other. It was Easton's turn.

"I'm afraid I don't understand."
"I don't either."

That makes three of us.

Jackie leaned over and looked into Browning's eyes.
"I wish you could talk."

Me too. I'd ask you what you're doing here.

Easton turned from the telephone.
"Excuse me?"
"Nothing."

Are you working this story for Time?

Easton began to dial. "I'll call Scotland Yard and see if they want me to send him to the Animal Shelter, or what."
"The Animal Shelter?"

The slammer?

Jackie stood to face Easton. "I could take him with me."
"Oh, my goodness, no. That would be impossible. One doesn't deceive Scotland Yard and get away with it. They may not believe me even now, but I'd rather face the music today with an honest mistake than tomorrow with deception written all over my face."
Suddenly the color drained from his face.
"Oh, my!"

Jackie turned to look at the desk where Browning had been sitting . . . but no longer was.

In the kitchen, the window curtains wafted lightly in the autumn breeze and Browning was gone.

9

Browning didn't notice the reaction of the two men when he got off the elevator by himself. He only noticed the chair. A big overstuffed chair covered in a soft gold plush-pile.

I loved that chair.

He turned and walked down the hall to his office and poked his head through the open doorway. Cardboard packing boxes were everywhere. Stacks of books, old magazines and newspapers cluttered the floor. Margaret was in a far corner, her back to the doorway, cleaning out a file cabinet.

Hello, Margaret.

He trotted quietly across the room into his inner office.

> *Cancel everything for the rest of the day and take all calls. I've gotta do some thinking.*

He turned and nudged the office door quietly shut.

Margaret began to sob quietly. She had just uncovered a photograph of Browning taken at a party some years before. He was wearing a Sherlock Holmes hat.

"Excuse me. Is Mr. Shackleton in?"

Margaret turned to the doorway.

"My name is Jackie Howard and I'd like to see him if I may."

Margaret sniffed and reached for her hankie. "I'm Mr. Shackleton. Mr. Browning always thought it looked better to have two names on the door. He said ours had a nice . . . ring . . . together."

Jackie took a step forward. "I'm sorry." For a moment, she considered coming back later but decided against it. Later these offices would be empty, the contents passed on to relatives, shipped to storage, sold at auction, or just thrown away. Things that might help in understanding why an *un*prominent, struggling private detective was involved with a *very* prominent designer and art collector who, in turn, was engaged to a member of Parliament.

Margaret sniffed.

Jackie took a deep breath.

"I know this is a terrible time but I would like to ask you a few questions. And I'd like to see Mr. Browning's office if that's possible."

Margaret glanced at Browning's closed office door, and sniffed again.

"I'm writing a book. Or rather I'm going to write a book. About what happened . . . or rather . . . *why* it happened."

Margaret glanced down at the photograph and began to sob. "It's my fault, you know. It's all my fault. The man on the phone made it sound so urgent. I thought I was doing the right thing."

She looked up at Jackie, her eyes now overflowing. "Mr. Browning wasn't even coming in that day until I called him. He was in bed with a terrible cold."

And she began to bawl. Instinctively Jackie moved to comfort her.

"You can't blame yourself."

Sniff.

"Yes I can."

"I'm sure it would have happened anyway."

Silent disbelief, then a new eruption of loud sobbing tears. What a dumb thing for me to say, thought Jackie.

"I'm sorry. I didn't mean that quite like it sounded." She spotted the photograph in Margaret's hand and tried to change the subject. "Is this Mr. Browning?"

Her heart skipped a beat. "Oh, my goodness."

Margaret looked up. And sniffed.

"What's the matter?"

"I know him . . . *knew* him."

Margaret turned to her desk.

Sniff.

"What is your name?"

Jackie gazed intently at the photograph.

"Jackie Howard."

Margaret flipped open a black ledger and turned a couple of pages.

Sniff.

"I'm afraid that's impossible."

"My name?"

"That you knew him. You'd be in the book."

"Oh! No . . . I had just met him. It must have been the day he was . . ."

A look from Margaret.

"It was pouring rain and I was chasing a bus and we sort of collided. He had this funny little red umbrella and I managed to fall on it and totally demolish it."

Margaret's grief erupted with new-found energy and Jackie reached for her and wrapped her in the comfort of a warm, understanding hug. She continued to gaze at the photograph over Margaret's shoulder.

"I didn't even know his name."

Margaret faced Jackie, finding strength in

what she now considered to be a joint despondence. Sniff.

"You'd like to see his office?"

"I'd like that very much."

Browning had just managed to unscrew the cap on the cough medicine bottle when the door opened and Margaret entered, followed by Jackie.

"He wanted people to think he was hard and unyielding, but he was just a puppy at heart."

The bottle cap dropped from Browning's mouth and he and Jackie stared at each other in blank shock. This was a bit more than coincidence could bear.

Sniff.

"Is this your dog?"

Jackie didn't hear. She was circling Browning in silent astonishment, trying to deal with an accelerating vertigo of rational reason.

"Miss Howard?"

Jackie just circled, gazing at Browning. Margaret feared the worst. She had once seen a possessed woman who had that same look in her eyes.

Jackie finally stopped circling and leaned across the desk, nose to nose with Browning, seeming to search his eyes for an answer.

Browning's heart beat faster.

You have the most beautiful eyes in the world.

"You're beginning to drive me crazy."

I know exactly how you feel.

"What are you doing here?"

Needed some cough medicine. What are you doing here?

Jackie took the bottle from between his paws, read the label, and sniffed the contents.

"This isn't cough medicine. It's . . . brandy!"

So I lied.

She recapped the bottle and set it on the desk.

"You might be a better story than the one I'm writing."

I think I am the one you're writing.

Sniff.

"Miss Howard? Are you all right?"

Jackie wandered across the room, then turned back, eyes fixed on Browning. After a long moment she looked at Margaret.

"You have no idea how strange this is."

"You should see it from here."

Jackie looked back to Browning. "Everywhere I go, he shows up."

"I see."

I was here first.

"Does he have something to do with your book?"

"No."

Book? I thought you wrote for Time.

Jackie tried to speak coherently, but she couldn't shake the enigma of Browning's presence.

"The book is . . . well . . . it's not about the actual murders themselves. . . ."

Margaret whimpered and reached for a tissue. Jackie apologized with a look.

"It's about the lives of three people, their emotions, their feelings, the event that brought them together and eventually led to such a . . . tragic end."

Jackie paused, studying a photograph on the wall. Browning and two British celebrities. And there was that feeling again. Like butterflies, but not quite. Calm, yet uneasy. Without knowing why, she turned from the photograph to look at Browning, but just for a moment; then she continued.

"Why, for example, would a socially prominent designer and art collector, engaged to a prominent member of Parliament, have an affair with an unprominent, struggling private detective?"

Sniff.

"He wasn't struggling . . . and there was no affair. The newspaper made that up. He didn't even know Patricia Elliot."

"Oh?"

Margaret opened a file drawer and, between sniffs, began stuffing its contents into a cardboard packing box.

"Unless, like you, he met her that day."

"How do you know?"

"Because she's not on the list."

"What list is that?"

Margaret gazed at the floor. "I kept a list of Mr. Browning's current lady friends."

It wasn't a list, just a couple of names.

Browning didn't know why but he didn't like Jackie hearing about the list. Never mind that he was dead. And a dog. Someone had neglected to inform his emotions of these changes.

"It was just in case something came up," Margaret continued. "I could always reach him at any time of day or . . . or whenever I needed to."

"I see," Jackie said. And the tone of her voice indicated that she did.

Browning sighed.

Margaret sniffed.

"Would you like to see it?"

Will you forget about the list?

"Yes, I would." Jackie dug around in her purse for her note pad and a pencil, dropped her recorder on Browning's desk, and followed Margaret toward the outer office. "I need to talk to anyone who has ever known any of the three people involved."

That could be helpful, Browning thought. She would be covering a lot of the same ground he needed to cover, only faster. And the man he was looking for might well be on her list.

Suddenly Jackie was back, looking at him from across the desk. "And in case you're planning any more surprises, when I leave here I'm going home. The Brockton Apartments. You know where it is."

She smiled as if she thoroughly expected him to understand, then wheeled around and walked out of the room.

If it's all the same, I think I'll ride this time. You do have your car, don't you?

He stretched, lay down on the desk top, closed his eyes, and spent the next hour contemplating whether or not Jackie Howard was the kind of person who allowed pets in bed with her.

10

Browning had never contemplated dog food before. Not seriously. The stuff looked awful. Like recycled meat loaf all globbed up in a bowl. And it smelled worse.

"Well, go ahead. Eat it."

Eat it? I wouldn't sit in it.

Browning just stared at the bowl.

"It's that or nothing." And Jackie wheeled and marched out of the kitchen.

Wrong.

He quietly stepped to the doorway and watched Jackie turn off a lamp in the living room and disappear into the bedroom. Then he turned and trotted defiantly to the refrigerater and scratched at the suction door, which opened easily. A veritable feast lay before him. Half a leftover roast. Salad fixings. Carrots, apples, cheese, and a half empty bottle of wine. Fantastic!

He was reaching for a piece of celery when his salivating was interrupted by a loud noise. He spun around toward the door. It sounded like running water. In a bath tub! Suddenly thoughts of food faded into the background of his consciousness.

He peered around the corner into the living room and looked across to the bedroom door.

> *Restraint, Browning. Exercise restraint.*

A shiver.

> *Don't be a nerd. How many guys get an opportunity like this?*

He raced into the living room, through Jackie's bedroom, and into the bathroom.

Yaaa haaa!!

SPLASH!

11

Browning sneezed loudly. Then sneezed again.

"Serves you right." Jackie was sitting at a small metal table thumbing through a note pad, and Browning sat next to her.

No regrets.

The room was completely unfurnished except for the small metal table and wooden benches on either side. There was nothing on the walls except institutional green. No pictures, no paintings, no artifacts. Nothing. And nothing on the single window opposite the table, except bars.

Browning had been inside a prison only once before. An official visit, courtesy of the state of Massachusetts. He had been accused of tampering with a witness in a legal action that could have cost Interline several million.

The witness was lying and Browning knew it, so he leaned on him a little. Not really blackmail, just encouragement toward the truth. The plaintiff screamed "foul" and Browning was thrown in the clinker.

A week later the witness broke down and told the truth and Browning was released, but that was probably the worst week he had ever spent in his life.

And this prison didn't look any different or smell any different than that one.

He shivered and tried to shake it off.

The door to the little room opened and three guards ushered a distinguished-looking man into the room. It was Quimby Charles.

Browning noted that a few days in jail had apparently left him none the worse for wear. Except for his wardrobe he looked pretty much like his picture in the paper. He must be a strong man, Browning thought. But he couldn't help feeling sorry for him. He knew what jail was like, especially when you didn't deserve to be there.

One guard remained in the room and the other two stood just outside the glass-paneled door. Jackie stood and extended her hand. "Mr. Charles. Thank you so much for seeing me."

Charles was cordial but cautious. He gave Jackie's hand a perfunctory shake.

"Miss Howard."

Then a glance to the dog.

"How did you manage that? Dogs are not

allowed. Seems there was a bad experience with one who liked to eat guards."

"I have special permission," Jackie said and glanced toward the grouping of guards around the door. "That's why we have so much company. I had hoped you would recognize him."

"Why ever would you hope that?"

"There is reason to believe he belonged to Patricia Elliot."

Charles stiffened a bit at the sound of her name.

"Patricia didn't have a dog. Why would you think she did?"

"I found him locked in her apartment."

Charles looked quizzically at Browning, and Browning turned and attempted to scratch himself innocently. Having never tried the hind-leg scratch before, Browning lost his balance and fell off the bench. He shook himself and climbed back onto his seat, trying to look as if nothing had happened.

Jackie punched on her recorder and flipped open her notebook, then allowed her gaze to fall onto Browning and for a moment she absorbed herself in the abstraction of unanswerable questions. It made Browning feel uneasy.

"Miss Howard?"

Jackie snapped back. "I'm sorry."

"There's a condition to this interview."

Jackie looked at him, a bit stunned.

"Oh?"

"Yes. My spies tell me that you are a good writer, an honest writer, and, most importantly, a thorough writer. You do a lot of research."

"All true."

"If I consent to this interview I want my attorneys to have access to your research."

Jackie just stared at him for a long blank moment. Then, finally: "I'm sorry . . . I . . ."

"Tapes . . . notes . . . photographs . . . anything that pertains to the case."

"Why wasn't I told this before I went to the trouble to come here?"

"Because I wanted you to hear the reason *why* from me."

"That much you accomplished. I'm listening."

Browning was watching the conversation like a tennis match, looking from one to the other. Charles sat quietly for a moment, studying Jackie. Browning figured he was calculating precisely how to proceed. His life might well depend on how he presented his case.

Browning couldn't help but admire his strength. He was a man not only accused of murder, but of having murdered the woman he loved. Yet he was realist enough to know that Patricia Elliot was gone and nothing he could do would bring her back. He also knew that if he was to have a future, he needed all the calm and stability he could muster right now. But then he had spent his life dealing with crises and was well programmed for it. A true politician, thought Browning, not really knowing whether he meant it negatively or positively.

Charles relaxed in his chair. "I didn't kill Patricia Elliot. I want to free myself of that charge *and* see the guilty party found. Your research might inadvertently turn up something that would help. It's that simple."

Jackie didn't want to get into it. This wasn't her story. Her story was about a man who murdered for love and the two people he murdered.

"Your fingerprints were on the murder weapon."

"It was a kitchen knife. I did most of the cooking."

"Then you were living with her?"

Charles paused, but never took his eyes off Jackie.

"I spent a great deal of time there."

"How did you meet her?"

He leaned back in his chair and seemed to enjoy another long pause.

"The condition, Miss Howard."

The twinkle in her eyes betrayed her appreciation of the checkmate. She thought she had him going but it was just bait. A tease. Jackie nodded.

"I agree."

"Good. I have only one more question."

He glanced toward Browning. "Is he always so attentive to conversations?"

Jackie took a long look at Browning. Someone

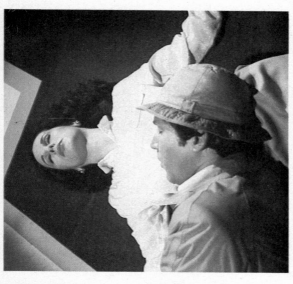

...but, as luck would have it, it _was_ his day. His _last_ day.

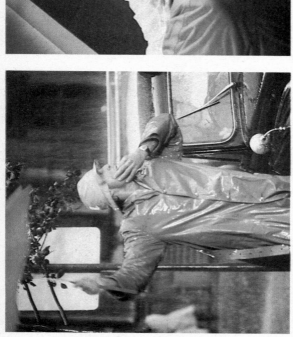

Browning suspects it just isn't his day when he wakes up with a terrible cold, it's pouring down rain, and he can't find a taxi...

"I'm afraid there's no mistake, Mr. Browning, that was definitely your natural termination time."

RRDD reminds Browning of a giant government office only it was all white.

Seeing himself as cute and fluffy was one thing, but seeing Freddie as a cat was more than Browning could handle.

Browning hears Malcolm Bart unexpectedly approaching.

Everyone has days they'd rather forget, but a calendar that skips from 14 to 16 just doesn't add up.

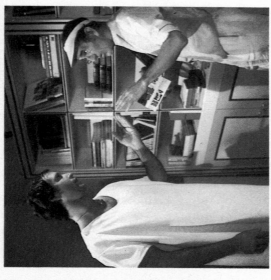

"I can't go back now," Browning insists. "The pieces are finally fitting together."

Browning discovers that his paws once again have fingers.

Malcolm Bart's sanity vanishes when he sees Browning snatch the envelope from Box 33.

Jackie's lunch with Alistair Becket is interrupted by an anxious Browning carrying the locket he knows will convict the real murderer.

Jackie and Browning are finally on the same level, so to speak.

else had noticed. But noticed what? "He seems to be . . . very bright."

The car suddenly screeched to a stop, sending Browning and the small black tape recorder tumbling to the floorboard.

Women drivers.

Jackie's voice continued to crackle through the little speaker. "But you were to be the next Prime Minister."

She reached for the recorder and placed it on the console as Quimby Charles's voice replied to her recorded comment: "It was possible. If the old man stepped down. If the party remained in power. The way things are, both are big ifs."

Jackie, recorded: "Especially if you're convicted."

Charles, recorded: "As I said, Miss Howard. I did most of the cooking but I did none of the killing."

Jackie jabbed at the stop button, then punched it into *record* and held the built-in microphone close to her mouth.

"So far my research can be summarized as follows: I'm told that Quimby Charles is innocent of killing Patricia Elliot who was *not* having an affair with a private detective who *didn't* know her. If that's all true, I have no story. If I have no story I have no book and it's back to *Time* magazine and I just wanted the little person inside this tape recorder to know that that really ticks me off!"

Click.

She dropped the recorder back onto the console and just drove for a long moment. Finally, she looked down at Browning. "That was a rotten thing to say, wasn't it?"

Browning didn't look up. He knew exactly how she felt, and the worst part of it was that she *didn't* have a story. Her big break was destined to go down the tubes and somehow that didn't quite seem fair.

He glanced up and she was still looking down at him.

> *Sorry. I have to disqualify myself. I have*
> *privileged information.*

Suddenly Jackie slammed on the brakes and Browning somersaulted onto the floor. Again.

He pulled himself back onto the seat and looked out to see the near miss. A silver Rolls, evacuating a parking place in front of the Needham Gallery.

> *The phone number on the calendar!*
> *Interesting how great minds work*
> *together.*

Jackie quickly parked and began rolling up the windows. Browning wondered why. It wasn't raining. As she stepped out of the car, he got his answer. "I'm afraid you'll have to sit this one out."

70

And the door shut in his face. Browning scratched and barked.

Wait a minute! Hey!!

Inside some fifty or sixty well-to-do art lovers were being served champagne and mingling amongst one of the most bizarre accumulations of sculpture ever brought together under one roof. Weird things resembling the man in Patricia Elliot's apartment, but worse. It was a room full of erotic mannequins molded in aluminum, many not all in one piece.

But the art itself was no stranger than the accumulation of patrons attending the showing. Haute bizarre, thought Jackie.

She stalked a very sweet man in a gold lamé jumpsuit. "I'm looking for the curator. A Mr. Edgeware?"

"Jeffrey? He's right over there. The one in the black tuxedo with the gold pinstriping."

Jackie thanked him and threaded her way through the strangies. Jeffrey Edgeware was a short pudgy man, apparently trying to hide his impish innocence behind a bushy black mustache.

"Mr. Edgeware? I'm Jacquelyn Howard. I spoke to you on the phone."

"Oh yes. About Miss Elliot."

His plaintively nasal little voice reminded Jackie of what an elf or a gremlin might sound like with a head cold. They began to stroll through the gallery toward the champagne table.

71

"She always attended our showings. In fact, Montanero was one of her favorites. She actually gave him his start several years ago when she bought his matched pair, *Adam and Eve*."

He handed Jackie a glass of champagne. "Would you like to meet him?"

"I would indeed . . ."

But their path was suddenly blocked by a loud, expensively overdressed bulge of a woman.

"Jeffrey, are you avoiding me?"

"Lady Chalmers, *there* you are!"

He grabbed Jackie by the arm. "I would like you to meet Miss Howard. She's writing a novel about the Patricia Elliot tragedy." Then, to Jackie, in a confidential whisper: "Patricia was redecorating Lady C's flat . . . when . . ."

"Yes! She was right in the middle of my vestibule. I don't know what to do. I am bereft."

Jackie blinked. "What a shame."

Jeffrey could only tolerate moments of Lady Chalmers at a time so he smiled his way out: "I'll see if I can find our artist while you ladies chat."

He vanished into the crowd and Lady Chalmers leaned toward Jackie's ear.

"Doesn't he wear dreadful cologne?"

Jackie blinked again. She hadn't noticed.

"Oh look! The Octavia sisters."

Jackie looked and had two immediate impressions. One, the Octavia sisters were pretty. Two, neither of them had been back to Earth in years.

They were strolling through the gallery in glazed-eye slow motion and in perfect sync with each other. Every step, every motion of the hand, every turn of the head.

"Do you know about the Octavia sisters? Of course you do. Everyone knows about the Octavia sisters. Oh, and *there's* Pamela Natwick. She came with *two* men."

Jackie knew it would be painful but she decided to question Lady Chalmers.

"Do you know Quimby Charles?"

"Oh darling, I know *everyone*."

Her sentence was punctuated by a loud sneeze. They both looked quizzically at the statue before them.

Another loud sneeze.

Jackie cringed, knowing very well what she was going to find when she looked under the drape at the base of the statue.

"Oh!" exclaimed Lady Chalmers. "A . . . dog!"

Browning smiled and wagged his tail.

You should talk.

Jackie tossed Browning back into the car, snapped a leash onto his collar, and tied it to the steering wheel.

"You embarrass me one more time and you'll find your cute fluffy little tail in the nearest animal shelter!"

She slammed the door and stalked away. Browning watched her for a moment, then turned and went to work on the knot with his teeth.

I don't like being cute. I don't like being fluffy. And I want two hands!

Montanero was a ruggedly handsome type with dark, wavy hair and an indistinguishable accent. He was just this side of bizarre, but not by much. A pair of western boots in lizard, a white silk peasant shirt, and an everyday tweed sportcoat appropriately crossed all lines of good taste. A single earring pierced his left ear.

He took two glasses of champagne from the waiter's tray and sat down on the couch. The twinkle in his eye reflected a keener interest in Jackie than in her questions.

"Anyway, I could count on selling at least one of my pieces every time she did someone's flat. Then quite suddenly she just dropped out of sight. But why don't we talk about it over cocktails?"

His hand *conversationally* landed on Jackie's knee and she pointedly handed it back to him.

"Please continue."

"I should really get back to my mingling. That's what I am supposed to do at these things. Mingle."

A long pause.

"Of course I would rather be here with you."

Jackie sighed a private sigh.

"Of course. What do you mean she just dropped out of sight . . ."

"I'm sorry. I really must pull myself away."

He stood up, then turned back. There was a long pause as he dangled himself and the information Jackie wanted before her. "Shall we say a late . . . candlelit snack . . . at my place?"

This kind was easy. And boring. But Jackie wanted his story.

"No. We'll say an early floodlit dinner at my place. Seven o'clock?"

He smiled and as quickly as he disappeared, Lady Chalmers took his place.

"Isn't he wonderful? I'd just love to love him."

She pulled Jackie to her feet and began dragging her across the room.

"Not so, of course, with Lord Heathwit. But still he wants to meet you and it can't hurt. He's twenty-seventh in line for the throne and really a darling little man. Blows bubbles when he talks, poor dear."

Suddenly she stopped in her tracks.

"Oh look. Alistair Becket!"

A tall handsome man in his late forties was moving through the large room from the entry foyer, speaking to everyone within range.

Lady Chalmers tried in vain to flatten out her various lumps then moved to attack Becket, dragging Jackie along like a child.

"He'll be our next Prime Minister you know, thanks to Quimby's . . . indiscretion. Isn't it fortunate he's so attractive? They're all so boring we might as well have one who is pleasant to look at."

She managed to block Becket's path, extending her hand.

"Alistair! Good to see you again."

Becket was very charming, with all the charisma of a politician on the brink of leadership, but it was obvious he didn't remember this one.

"Yes . . . uhh . . ."

"Lady Chalmers. We were introduced by Lady Alcott."

Still nothing.

"Of course."

"I believe you met her in Switzerland. She said she found you schussing down a slope. That is the word, isn't it? Schussing? It sounds so naughty . . ."

Becket's attention wandered. He reached for Jackie's hand. "How do you do. I'm Alistair Becket."

"I know."

Lady Chalmers didn't miss a beat. "Oh, I do apologize. This is Jacquelyn Howard. She's writing a book about Patricia and Quimby and that detective."

"Oh? What kind of book?"

His interest seemed quite genuine and Jackie marveled at how most politicians can create such an illusion.

"A good one, I hope."

Elsewhere in the gallery, a handsome young man in a three-piece suit was stalking toward the front door, pursued by a girl with a Medusalike

76

headful of very thin braids flopping around her head like a bunch of garden snakes.

"But you don't have to *understand* it, you just have to *feel* it."

The man stopped at the door and smiled sweetly: "I do *feel* it. That's why we're leaving."

He opened the door and a small, brown ball of cute-and-fluffy darted between his feet, dragging a chewed half-a-leash behind him.

Browning disappeared into a sea of legs and feet, moving unnoticed into the gallery, searching face after face for someone or something familiar. Any kind of a clue. But all he saw were strange people and weird sculptures.

This guy is sick.

He paused near a low table . . . and a glass of champagne, easily within his reach. It seemed like months since he had a drink. A real drink. And no one seemed to be looking.

He stepped up to the glass and lapped a sip, when suddenly, across the room, he saw the man he had been looking for. A fleeting glance because somebody stepped in the way.

He scrambled for a better look and got one that jerked him to a stop. It was indeed the man who had hired him, sitting on a couch . . . talking to Jackie!

He eased closer, from behind Jackie, straining to hear their conversation, protected in the knowledge that the man couldn't recognize his current disguise.

But he did. Or seemed to, stopping in mid-sentence with a look at Browning that would chill an Eskimo.

What is he looking at me for?! He's never seen me in this suit.

Jackie turned to see what the man was staring at and spotted Browning.

A sigh.

"BJ, come here!"

BJ did, reluctantly.

"Is this your dog?"

Browning was thoroughly baffled and a bit nervous at the way the man was looking at him.

"On occasion," said Jackie, toying with the chewed end of the leash.

Back to the interview.

"Anyway . . . you were saying that you first met Patricia Elliot at a showing like this. How long ago was that?"

The man looked at his watch. "I'm sorry. I really have to go. Perhaps we can continue this another time."

And he abruptly picked up his coat and left. Browning struggled to get away. He didn't want to lose track of him now, but Jackie had both hands around his neck.

"Will you be still? You're becoming more trouble than you're worth!"

She continued to scold him but he made no attempt to be attentive, alternately straining to see where the man had gone and looking for a way out of her strangle hold. He caught a glimpse of the tape recorder in her lap and stretched a hind foot to give it a nudge . . . and it crashed to the floor. Jackie dove for the recorder and Browning was gone.

He spotted the man going through the front door and raced after him, but too late. The door was shut tight. He scratched frantically but it seemed that no matter which side of a door a dog was on, everyone assumed he was *supposed* to be there. He glanced quickly around the entry foyer.

> *What does it take to get thrown out of this place?*

Then he saw his answer. A short sculpture in the corner. He dashed over to it, barked once, and lifted his leg. A dozen hands grabbed for him.

He sailed through the door and hit the ground at full speed. The man was nearly a block away now, disappearing around a corner. Dodging pedestrians like a halfback, Browning raced down the sidewalk and skidded around the same corner as fast as his little legs would carry him. Then suddenly:

> *Ohhh rats!*

And he reappeared running for his life, pursued by a teeth-gnashing monster of a dog at least ten times his size. The carnivorous giant galloped blindly up the street right past Browning, huddled in the dark shadows of a narrow alcove.

Big but dumb.

And, like a flash, he bolted back down the sidewalk and around the corner.

At the end of the next block he came to a panting stop. The man was nowhere in sight.

I don't believe it.

He had lost him. The key to the entire setup. Possibly even the murderer himself.

I just don't believe it.

Disgustedly, he turned to retrace his steps and suddenly jarred into a man's leg. He looked up into the stony face of the very man he was chasing. The man who hired him. The man from the gallery.

"If I didn't know better I'd swear you were following me."

Browning instinctively took a step backwards.

What? Me? A dog. How could I be following you?

The man followed, looming over him like a giant. He called to Browning, trying to sound friendly.

"Come here. Here, doggy."

Sorry. I've gotta be running along.

Browning tried to bolt away but the man snared his left hind leg and almost jerked it out of the socket as he yanked him back and began a search through his fur. Browning was scared. This could be the end of the line. Again.

The man looked in his ears, mouth, checked his collar, then roughly flipped him onto his back. He hit with a thump and it hurt. Another thump. But he didn't feel that one. He opened his eyes to see a little old lady, seething in righteous indignation, whacking the man with an umbrella.

"You let go of him!!"

Stunned and embarrassed, the man did as he was told. Browning bolted for the corner, then peered back to watch his assailant hurry off across the street.

How could that creep suspect I'm anything but a normal dog?

The man obviously did, however, and that meant he was dangerous. And that could cramp Browning's style.

He watched the man dissolve into the London crowd across the street and was pondering the risk of continued pursuit when he heard a deep, booming bark. He spun to look up the sidewalk. It was the same huge dog that had chased him earlier and was coming for Browning.

I don't need this!

He dove around the corner, the big dog in hot pursuit.

12

Jackie knew she would have trouble with Easton. He was afraid of his own shadow. But she didn't expect the door to be slammed in her face. She knocked again.

"I just want to make a list of her clients. I won't touch anything but the files, I promise."

Nothing.

She was having more trouble than she had anticipated finding people to talk to about Patricia Elliot. Other than the pompous patrons and the strangies at Needham Gallery, she could find no one who knew her. No one sane, that is. No one sensitive enough to be able to tell her what Patricia Elliot was really like.

She pounded on the building manager's door.

"You could get the list for me!"

The door flew open and Easton's head poked out.

"I said *no* one. That includes me! They were very upset about the dog getting away and they sealed the flat shut. *No* one is allowed inside until after the trial."

SLAM!

Jackie sighed and walked outside, almost tripping over a fluffy yellow cat. She didn't notice the cat, or the brass disc hanging around his neck.

13

He was a mixed-breed giant. Tall enough to look into a garbage can without lifting a foot off the ground, and big enough not to fit.

He methodically sniffed through the piles of rubbish, cardboard boxes, and trash cans, seeming to know that Browning was somewhere in the vicinity.

He was right. Browning was shivering quietly amongst the garbage at the bottom of one of the taller cans.

Dear Mom. It all started when I was lying in bed with this bad cold . . . and the phone rang. . . .

14

To call this restaurant plush would be like describing a Rolls-Royce as *sort of nice*. Chic. *Très* chic. The kind with more waiters and bus boys than customers.

The portly English gentleman who had been with Jackie in Paris was now sitting across the table from her. He hung up the phone.

"I shan't repeat what they said, although I'm sure you've heard language like that before. Suffice to say the answer was no."

A waiter unplugged the telephone and removed it from the table, while another placed a *trés* chic dessert in front of each of them and a third refilled their long-stemmed, *trés* chic wine glasses. This was a working lunch, with an agenda, several manuscripts, and a couple of books stacked on the table. And from the attention the gentleman was getting, one would deduce it was a daily affair.

"Bernie, I need that client list."

Bernie had a spoonful of Strawberries Alouette in one hand and a small piece of English cheddar in the other.

"Then I suggest you find someone with friends at the Yard."

He tossed the cheese into his mouth and reached for a book. "Inasmuch as this has now hit the bestseller list, I'm afraid I have only enemies."

The book was entitled: *Weeds in the Yard — Scotland Yard's Greatest Blunders*.

Jackie sank back in her chair and stared off into space.

"I saw Quimby Charles today."

Bernie wiped whipped cream from his mouth. "So?"

"I think I believe he's innocent."

A bite of cheese. "Don't get distracted, Jackie."

"He's very convincing."

Another strawberry. "He's a politician. It goes with the job."

"You're a cynic."

A dab with the napkin. "How could anyone get to my age and not be? Besides . . ."

"I know. It goes with the job."

15

Browning was trying desperately to stifle an oncoming sneeze, but the stench in the garbage can combined with his latent cold was making any hope of repressing it impossible. It came. A loud one.

The sound rang off the metal walls of the can and instantly two giant paws hit the rim above. The big dog glared down at Browning, his huge, ugly head taking up most of the opening.

> *Does it matter that I've already been killed this week and you aren't gonna be first?*

A thundering bark flattened Browning into a crumpled heap.

I didn't think so.

The huge dog lunged against the side of the can, crashing it into the pavement, and once again the chase was on.

16

The late afternoon sun was peeking through the boiling London clouds for the first time in days, as Jackie drove in and turned her car over to the doorman.

"George, have you seen that little dog that was with me this morning?"

"No, ma'am. Is he lost again?"

Jackie looked at him blankly for a long moment, then shrugged. "I haven't the faintest idea."

She turned for the door. "If he shows up, please let him in and buzz me."

Evening.

Stars twinkled in the crisp night air as a silver Lotus with green trim and a bright red apple as a hood ornament roared into the entry drive of Jackie's apartment. A man wearing a dark blue velvet jacket and silver ascot got out and swaggered into the lobby. Moments later, Browning turned the corner, only a step ahead of the big dog who was now following happily along, tail wagging like a puppy.

> *So you see it's just a matter of communication. Even with vast differences between two individuals there can still be shared experiences . . . a meeting of the minds . . .*

He glanced up at the big dog trotting beside him.

> *. . . and if you've got a mind I'd certainly like to meet it.*

The big dog slobbered good-naturedly at Browning's glance, but Browning didn't notice. He had his eye on the target. The doorway into the lobby. And the doorman standing next to it.

> *For Pete's sake, please remember me.*

He glanced back at the big dog.

> *Well this is it. Let's get together again real soon.*

And he picked up speed and headed straight for the entrance. The door obligingly opened, Browning trotted through followed by the doorman, and the door closed, leaving the big dog whining outside.

Browning exhaled a sigh of relief.

Jackie was more beautiful than ever. Her hair was down, long and silky and flowing softly over her shoulders. She was wearing a loose, netty sort of dress that, when the light was just right, made her look like an angel.

But she wasn't very pleased with Browning.

"Where have you been? You smell awful!"

She took Browning from an unhappy doorman, thanked him, and nudged the door shut.

"Did you spend the day in a garbage dump?"
She dropped him to the floor.

Close. Who's the weirdo with the ear bob?

Montanero was sitting on the couch, sipping a glass of wine. In a blue velvet jacket and a silver ascot. And suddenly Browning felt incredibly jealous. Jackie returned to the couch.

"So, there was no one special in her life?"

"Well, I cannot speak for the year she was away. But before . . . and after . . . she saw many different men."

"She what?"

"Saw many different men."

I don't believe this. Who is this creep?
I couldn't have been that wrong. Surely
Jackie's got better taste. He's got the only
Italian accent I've ever heard with a
Texas twang.

91

Browning jumped on the couch and settled down between them. Montanero quickly grabbed him and dropped him to the floor.

"Always someone else," he went on.

"Is not my way," Montanero continued. "I am . . . monogamous."

Browning looked him square in the face.

You are ridiculous!

"With me there can be only one."

Montanero's hand accidently landed on Jackie's knee . . . and with a pouncing leap Browning landed on his hand!

He jerked it away and Jackie promply filled it with her empty wineglass, smiled, and stood up.

"Would you mind, I'll get the hors d'oeuvres."

She disappeared into the kitchen and Montanero immediately dropped his charming smile, picked up Browning, and threw him halfway across the room.

"Go away. You stink." Then he got up and went to the bar, stopping long enough to stomp a foot at Browning.

"I said go away."

And he stomped his foot again.

You're asking for it, greasy.

Montanero uncorked the wine bottle and began pouring, then suddenly fired a horrified look toward the floor. Browning's leg was cocked over his shoe.

"Hey!!"

Browning took off across the room, pursued. Twice around the couch, back to the bar, behind the chair, and finally under the table.

When Jackie stopped in the doorway, all she could see of Montanero was his rear end, poking out from under the table.

"What are you doing?"

Montanero scooted back on his stomach and looked up at her, taking several moments to consider the situation. Finally, a smile. "I just dropped my napkin."

They resituated themselves on the couch and Jackie continued to fire questions at him.

"So. Patricia was gone for a year. Where had she been?"

"She would not speak of it. Jeffrey heard that she was somewhere in Switzerland. But it was just a rumor."

"How did she seem when she showed up again? I mean, was she the same Patricia?"

"I'm sorry. I cannot concentrate. Being around you makes me feel . . . I don't know . . . like I've never felt before. I know that sound like a . . . string."

"A line."

". . . a line. But it is not. I am being honest . . ."

His hand found its way back to her knee and began to rub it.

"I have such trouble expressing my feelings . . . except in my work . . ."

The hand continued, gaining confidence.

"But you make me want to say things, . . . and do things . . ."

He made a move . . . but found Browning's head, now nestled snugly and strategically in Jackie's lap.

Montanero smiled dumbly.

"Nice doggie."

"I'd say so," Jackie smiled. "He just saved your life."

17

Jackie's tape recorder barely survived its crash to the floor in Needham Gallery and was now held together with assorted pieces of masking tape. The injured machine was nestled comfortably on a soft cushioned stool and its cassette played semingly without effort. Next to the stool Jackie was totally absorbed in a luxurious bubble bath as her conversation with Alistair Becket droned from the little speaker.

Jackie, recorded: ". . . so it's not really the story of the tragedy itself, more the story behind the tragedy . . . whatever it is.

Becket, recorded: "I beg your pardon?"

Jackie, recorded: "Do you believe Quimby Charles is guilty?"

Becket, recorded: "I suppose that question is

best left up to a jury. I actually haven't given it much thought."

Jackie, recorded: "Not to be impertinent, Mr. Becket, but that's a bit difficult to believe. Hasn't the entire affair more or less guaranteed your trip to Number Ten Downing Street?"

Becket, recorded: "My, my, Miss Howard. Propriety is not one of your virtues."

There was a long pause, then: "My apologies."

"Accepted. How else can I help?"

"Did you know Patricia Elliot?"

"Not really, just passing acquaintances. But we did know a lot of the same people, so if I, or my office, can be of any assistance with your research, please don't hesitate to call on me."

"That's very kind. Thank you."

Jackie punched off the recorder and stretched her long slender leg down the length of the tub, her foot disappearing beneath a mound of suds.

The mound of suds sneezed.

18

Alistair Becket's secretary was sitting upright at her desk like a stone soldier guarding the castle gate.

"I'm sorry. Mr. Becket can not be interrupted for another hour. This is his *think* time."

Jackie was standing across the desk with Browning on his leash, now shorter because the two chewed ends had been knotted back together.

"You don't seem to be listening. He told me to interrupt him whenever I needed his help. And I need it now. It will only take a matter of minutes. I assure you."

"I'm sorry. It's out of the question. You may leave your name, or come back later, or whatever you like."

Jackie was seriously considering pulling the woman's hair out when a door opened and

Becket stepped out with a stack of papers. He immediately responded to Jackie.

"Oh, hello. I didn't know we'd be seeing each other again so soon."

"I need a small favor . . . but if you'd rather, I'll come back later."

Becket didn't hesitate.

"No, no, no. Please come in."

To the secretary: "Hold my calls." Which, of course, went straight to the heart and she was visibly stung. Becket ushered Jackie and Browning into his office and shut the door. He offered Jackie a seat and retreated to the chair behind his desk.

"Cute dog."

And fluffy.

"What can I do for you?"

Becket's office was large but comfortable and conservatively decorated except for a sculpture of a woman standing in one corner. A *bizarre* sculpture of a woman. Very much like the man Browning had seen in Patricia Elliot's flat.

I can't stand it. Montanero's stuff all over the world.

As the conversation continued between Jackie and Becket, Browning surveyed the room. On the wall immediately behind the desk, was a large family portrait of Becket, his wife, and two children.

"I don't know," Jackie was saying. "Maybe nothing. Scotland Yard has impounded Patricia Elliot's flat and I need very much to have a look at her client files . . . to set up interviews. I need names and addresses and phone numbers . . . and, well, I thought maybe you might know someone who knew someone. . . ."

"I see . . ."

On the wall behind the statue was a pair of antique wooden skis hanging next to a painting of the Swiss village of Zermatt, with the Matterhorn looming behind.

There was a long and studied pause while Becket considered. Browning scanned a large bookshelf, then stood on his hind legs, trying to see the top of Becket's desk. Jackie swatted at him.

"BJ, get down."

Becket hit the intercom.

"Malcolm would you come in here, please."

From the intercom speaker: "Yes, sir."

Becket turned back to Jackie. "My administrative assistant is good at this sort of thing. He can probably come up with something."

The door opened and Browning's heart leaped into his throat. Malcolm Bart, Alistair Becket's personal assistant, was the man from the gallery! The man who hired him to protect Patricia Elliot! The phony Quimby Charles!

Bart's face tightened and Browning backed away from his icy stare.

*He knows something. Otherwise he
wouldn't look at me that way. But why?
How?*

Browning wrapped himself in the ,safety of
Jackie's legs.

*Surely he wouldn't try anything in front
of these people. They'd think he was
crazy. He probably is. Maybe he just
hates dogs! But how can this man know
anything? Are there traitors in heaven?*

"Miss Howard, this is Malcolm Bart . . ."

"Yes, I met Mr. Bart at the gallery yesterday."

Bart's reaction to Browning was merely a
flicker, recognized by no one except the little dog.
Bart was now all charm. He approached Jackie
and shook her hand.

"Nice to see you again. Did you enjoy the
show?"

"It was . . . different."

Thoughts raced through Browning's head, his
heart thumping like a drum. Becket's voice was
fading into the Background.

"Miss Howard is writing a book about Quimby,
Patricia Elliot, and that detective . . . the murders
and all that . . ."

The lady sculpture. Patricia Elliot's man sculpture. *Adam and Eve.* That's what the gallery
curator had said on tape. Patricia Elliot had
bought Montanero's matched pair, *Adam and
Eve.*

He glanced back at the painting from Switzerland. Montanero said Patricia Elliot's year away from London was rumored to be in Switzerland. She said she found you schussing down a slope.

And Malcolm Bart. No coincidence there. He definitely hired Browning to protect a girl who was dead when he arrived. There was no question to Browning he had been totally and neatly set up. But why? The thoughts ran faster. He wondered where Becket was during the year Patricia Elliot wasn't in London. How many times he went to Switzerland. Or if he had a place in Switzerland. Or how much danger Jackie was getting into without even realizing it?

Bart was smiling. "I think we can work something out. Do you mind if someone from Scotland Yard is present when you look at the files?"

"Not at all," said Jackie.

"Then there should be no problem. I should have an answer by tomorrow."

And if there's anything to see, it'll be gone by then, right?

Becket stood, signaling the end of the meeting. "Good. Check with me around mid-morning."

Jackie stood up and moved toward the door with Browning in tow.

"I really appreciate this. I hope I can return the favor. . . ."

Becket smiled. "No return necessary, Miss Howard. It's my pleasure."

"Thank you."

The door shut behind her and Becket just stared at nothing for a long moment . . . then turned to Bart.

"Don't worry," Bart said. "I'll take care of it."

19

It was night before Browning could finally get away from Jackie and make his way across to Patricia Elliot's apartment. He leaped onto one of the garbage cans next to the fire escape, but the lid flipped and he fell into the can.

PLOP. Right on top of a fluffy, yellow cat who screeched in horror and sprung seven feet straight into the air, landing safely outside on another can.

Browning's head popped up out of the can. "Freddie?"

"Really, Benjamin, you have no finesse at all."

"Sorry. Your tail wasn't out."

"Smooth talker."

Browning pushed through the kitchen door into Patricia Elliot's living room, pausing to take a long look at the statue of the man.

Adam and Eve. No question about it.
Just like I've always pictured them.

And he trotted on into the studio.

Now what am I looking for and where
would it be?

He glanced around the room. At nothing.
Books, pictures, swatches of fabric . . . and the
self-closing closet! He had forgotten about that.
He moved to the door and pushed on it, then
scratched trying to open it. It was shut tight. But
it had been open the day Jackie and Easton came
in. And it closed *itself*. Somebody had been in
there. Had to be.

He walked away from the door, then it hit
him.

Bart!

He spun the events of that day through his
mind.

Of course. That would explain
everything. Little wonder he's crazy
if he watched a dog make a phone call.

Browning glanced at the desk, then the tall
three-drawer file cabinet.

Maybe Becket's in the files.

The top drawer was the target. Labeled A-F.
He started working his way up, first onto the
desk chair, then the desk, around the back table

to the file cabinet, then suddenly he froze. Someone was coming in the front door. He scrambled to the floor and dove under the desk.

Browning listened as the footsteps crossed the living room, paused, entered the studio, and finally stopped near the file cabinet. He stretched for a peek and confirmed his suspicion. It was Malcolm Bart.

Bart rummaged through the top drawer of the file cabinet, withdrew a thick folder, and idly moved to the desk.

Browning's heart began to pound as the man dropped down into the desk chair, his feet coming to rest only inches from Browning's cold, wet nose.

The foot tapped nervously as Bart sifted through the contents of the folder. Then a leg stretched into the corner and Browning jumped to one side, sitting straight up on his hind legs to avoid contact. One touch, one bump, and there was no one here to protect him. No Jackie. No old lady with an umbrella. The other foot advanced and began to tap on Browning's hind paw. He was as petrified as he had ever been in his life. Then suddenly Bart stood up.

He folded several papers, stuck them into his coat pocket, returned the folder to the file drawer, and left the room.

Browning listened as Bart closed the front door behind him, then he eased out from under the desk.

Flash!

Suddenly the room was flooded with light, and Browning fell all over himself scrambling back under the desk.

More footsteps, walking toward Browning. His blood was no longer flowing. His heart had stopped. This was it. Bart knew he had been under the desk all along and he was just toying with him. Now he had come back for the kill.

He saw a pair of legs. But no black overcoat. These legs were wearing white pants.

"I'm sorry, Mr. Browning, I didn't mean to startle you."

A New England accent. Then he saw the face that went with the voice. It was Mr. Higgins from IDEF!

"Mr. Higgins?"

Browning suddenly felt that he was consuming the entire knee hole under the small desk. Stuffed and puffy. He looked down and saw a white hospital gown. He was back in human form!

Overjoyed, he crawled out from under the desk and leaped to his feet.

"Higgins, I love you! You don't know how much I need this!"

He made a bee-line for the file cabinet.

"I'm afraid it's only temporary, Mr. Browning. Just while I'm here. Makes it easier for conversation."

"I should have known. You didn't answer my question. What are you doing here?" Browning was withdrawing the B folder from the top file drawer.

"I thought you would like to know about the mix-up."

Browning slammed the file folder shut.

"No Becket. There was something here and that creep took it."

He looked at Higgins.

"What mix-up?"

"It's highly unusual and I don't understand how it happened, but the clerk in RRDD gave you a limited Returnable. It has to be back by noon tomorrow."

Browning couldn't believe it. He hit the ceiling.

"That wench!"

"*Please*, Mr. Browning! We understand the problem! We just haven't been able to find the proper solution."

"Well I'm not it! And I'm not going back until I'm finished!"

He slammed the file drawer shut and headed for the door. Higgins followed.

"I'm afraid you have no choice unless you want to remain here until the dog's natural termination time."

Browning burst through the kitchen door with Higgins right on his heels.

"Things are just beginning to happen! The pieces are finally fitting together!"

"I'm sorry, Mr. Browning . . ."

Browning spun around. "This is not a time for

confession, it's a time for action. Now go get me an extension or something." He slapped open the window and started climbing through.

"I've gotta run. Turn off the lights when you leave."

Outside, Browning, now a small dog again, scrambled through the kitchen window and down the metal steps.

The lights in Patricia Elliot's apartment blinked off.

20

Ri-i-ing; Ri-i-ing!

The white and gold telephone glistened in a slice of morning sunlight.

Ri-i-ing! Ri-i-ing!

Jackie rolled over, still asleep, and fumbled around on the nightstand for the receiver.

Ri-i-ing! Ri-i-i . . .

Contact. The receiver disappeared into the fluff of Jackie's pillow and she mumbled a sleepy, "Hello." Then, like she had been hit with a bucket of cold water, she bolted upright in bed.

"What?"

Alistair Becket was in his office on the other end of the line. "I said I have your dog. It seems the security guard found him wandering the halls last night."

Browning was on a nearby couch, his head lying between his two front paws. Disgusted.

"That's the one, cute and fluffy."

Browning gave him a look.

Bite a banana.

Becket hung up the phone and immediately his secretary's voice crackled through the intercom: "Your nine o'clock meeting is here."

"Send them in. And when Miss Howard arrives, her dog will be in Bart's office."

Outside, the London traffic was unusual for early morning. Nose-to-tail. Chock-a-block. A black taxi worked its way to the curb and Bart got out. He paid the driver and hurried into the House of Parliament.

Jackie rushed through the apartment lobby buttoning her blouse with one hand and combing her hair with the other.

"I don't need this aggravation. I can't write my book. I can't get any rest . . . and I'm talking to myself!"

"Yes, mum," said the doorman as he opened the door and stood back. Jackie didn't hear him but he was used to it. He smiled politely at the departing taxi.

Bart's office was pathologically neat, the product of a supremely ordered mind. But it was a break for Browning. He was alone . . . and looking. There had to be something tangible to tie Becket to Patricia Elliot's death. There *had* to be. Browning was head-deep in a desk drawer when he heard Bart's voice in the office outside.

"Good morning, Nancy."

"Good morning, Mr. Bart."

Bart took off his coat and reached for the door to his office.

"Oh, Mr. Bart. Mr. Becket asked that you join him. He wanted you to meet the Ambassador."

Bart hesitated, then crossed the room to Becket's office and went in. Browning breathed a sigh of relief. He shut the drawer and jumped into Bart's chair to survey the top of the desk. He pawed through some papers. Nothing. Parliamentary business. He nosed open a file folder, then leafed through a legal pad. Still nothing. A note scrawled on Bart's desk calendar caught his eye: BECKET'S BIRTHDAY, RATHBONE ST. & WENTWORTH RD.

Browning wondered what Becket would do if one of his birthday presents were a bloody kitchen knife. His pleasure at the thought might be why he didn't hear Bart enter the room. And Bart didn't see Browning, at first. When he did, he exploded.

"Hey!"

The shock sent Browning spilling off the chair, pulling the calendar and legal pad with him. Bart lunged across the office and dove for Browning under the desk. He didn't see Jackie enter the room.

"BJ? Are you in here?"

Bart jerked his head up, crashing it into the drawer above — which, in turn, caused a spontaneous release of his grasp on Browning's throat.

"Mr. Bart. Is that you?"

Jackie rushed around the desk.

"Oh! Did BJ do this? I'm so sorry." She began cleaning up the mess. "He has been absolutely nothing but trouble since the first time . . ." She was flipping the calendar pages back to the correct date and the birthday note caused the pause.

"Oh, is today Mr. Becket's birthday?"

Bart handed Browning back to Jackie.

"I think you'd better go."

Jackie tried a friendly chuckle. "Maybe he'd like a dog for a present."

Bart took her arm and firmly ushered her toward the door. She tried again. "I'm really sorry about all this."

Bart's expression didn't change. Sort of glazed-over. He held the door open for her to leave.

In the outer office Becket was returning a set of files to his secretary. He looked up and smiled cautiously.

"Hello, Jackie."

Jackie had hoped she wouldn't see him. She felt her face flush with embarrassment.

"I apologize for the trouble."

"No trouble."

He started for his office, then turned back. "Malcolm should have an answer from Scotland Yard this morning. Why don't we meet for lunch and I'll give you the verdict."

Jackie was moving toward the door with Browning in her arms.

"Thank you. I'd love to."

"Good. How about Chez Revien? Twelve-thirty?"

She opened the door to leave.

"Perfect. I'll buy you a birthday drink."

Becket's face went blank.

"Birthday drink?"

Browning was certain he saw Bart exhale a tiny sigh of disgust.

"Yes . . . uhh . . . isn't today your birthday?"

"Not even close. My birthday is the third of March. Three three."

In perfect sync, Jackie and Browning looked toward Bart's office. The door was now shut.

Weird.

Browning was suddenly very curious about the intersection of Rathbone Street and Wentworth Road.

"I thought I saw a note on the desk in there but I guess I misread it." She knew she hadn't.

"So I'll buy you a non-birthday drink."

"I accept."

21

The intersection of Wentworth Road and Rathbone Street was right in the middle of the worst possible section of London. And a shiny black limousine looked out of place.

It stopped at the curb and the driver got out, walked around the car, and opened the back door. Browning jumped to the sidewalk and trotted off.

Thanks, Hermione.

A bejewelled elderly lady peered out at Browning through a pair of glasses on a stack. Encased in a crystal and diamond pendant hanging from a gold chain around her neck was . . . a returnable tag.

"Do be careful, Mr. Browning. You know this is not one of the better parts of our London."

The driver gave her a hopeless look, shut the door, climbed in, and drove away.

Browning glanced around the intersection. A couple of shops, a boarded-up warehouse, an auto garage, and an old post office.

So what does this have to do with Becket's birthday . . . which was six months ago . . . or six months from now, depending on how you look at it.

Probably nothing.

That's stupid. It's gotta mean something. Why would Bart make a note about a birthday half-a-year from the date in question?

He just stood for a moment, gazing up at the post office.

Hmmm.

It was small and run-down, but apparently in operation. The front door was ajar.

Becket's birthday.

Pause.

Nahhh.

Pause.

Why not?

He trotted up the stairs into the building.

Because it's too obvious, that's why.

Inside, he gazed up at a bank of post office boxes.

Not necessarily.

He walked slowly down the battery of little glass doors, each numbered, each with its own combination lock.

Someone would have to see Bart's calendar and know Becket's birthday was March 3rd, come down here and find a post office box and then put two and two together.

Or in this case three and three.

He was staring up at post office box number 33. It was on the top row and there was an envelope inside.

Now how do I get to it?

Outside, a taxi pulled up . . . and Malcolm Bart got out.

Browning jumped onto the counter and peered through one of the barred windows. Two young men were moving toward the back door and an older man was sorting letters against a far wall. The taller of the two stopped at the door and called to the old man: "Hey, Pop, we're going to lunch."

There was no response.

"Pop!! We're going to lunch now!!"

The old man still didn't respond. The two young clerks laughed and disappeared through the swinging metal door.

Browning slipped through the bars of the window and sneaked quietly along the narrow inside counter. Quietly until a rack of rubber stamps fell to the floor with a clatter. Browning spun and froze.

Confounded tail.

The old man didn't look up from his sorting.

The taxi drove away and Malcolm Bart just stood in the middle of the empty street for a long moment before turning and walking toward the post office. Like the limousine, he and his tailored tweed topcoat looked out of place against the backdrop of broken buildings and littered sidewalks.

Meanwhile, Browning was discovering that climbing is not a dog's strong suit. He was struggling up a stack of mail sacks, trying to reach the ledge above the post office boxes. Why couldn't he have been a cat? No, why couldn't he have been a *person*? His *own* person?

He leaped across to the ledge and scurried down the wall toward number 33.

Bart was also moving toward 33. He reached for the combination lock and suddenly froze in disbelief. On the other side, a dog's mouth was reaching for the envelope. For a split second they just looked at each other, then Browning jammed his nose further into the box and grabbed at the envelope.

He was hanging from the ledge, upside down, with his head crammed into the box to his ears. Bart was frantically working on the lock. Browning missed the envelope and tried again. The glass door swung open and Browning snatched the envelope away only inches ahead of Bart's hand.

He tried to scramble back onto the ledge but he was off balance and almost fell.

Suddenly Bart's entire arm punched through the box, blindly snared Browning's front leg, and flipped him off the ledge. His shoulder twisted as the weight of his body jerked against the man's steel grip. Pain! Like a red-hot spike!

He was dangling helplessly in midair with the envelope clenched in his teeth. Bart screamed for the clerk.

"Hello in there! Can someone help me?!"

The old man looked up from his sorting, not sure whether he heard something or not. He decided he didn't, and because Browning was dangling out of sight around the corner, nothing seemed amiss, and so he turned back to his table.

Bart screamed again, even louder, and this time the clerk climbed out of his chair and tottered toward one of the barred windows.

Browning struggled violently but couldn't wriggle out of Bart's grasp. Finally, in desperation, he dropped the envelope and viciously attacked the hand that held him. Bart screeched and

Browning dropped to the floor. He snapped up the envelope and raced for the back door.

Bart met the old clerk at the window.

"Stop that animal!!"

The clerk smiled politely.

"Stamps with animals? Yes, I believe we do," he answered calmly. "But you don't have to shout."

Bart's eyes were bulging and his face was ruby-red with rage, but he could only watch as Browning disappeared through the swinging metal door at the back of the building.

22

Browning trotted out of the elevator, the envelope still gripped in this teeth. He walked two steps ahead of an obviously contemptuous doorman who was doing his job, but wasn't at all happy about it. He begrudgingly admitted Browning into Jackie's flat.

Inside, Browning dropped the envelope on the floor and ripped it open with his teeth. A gold pendant slid out, small and delicate, engraved with the shape of a mountain peak. It hung on a thin gold chain.

What on earth is that?

He picked it up with his tongue and turned it over. The letters *ALP* were engraved on the back.

> *I refuse to believe the people I'm dealing with are that redundant.*

He paced idly across the room.

Why would anyone write alp on an alp??

He glanced back at the pendant.

*Love-y things go on pendants. Like Andy
loves Polly . . .*

He walked back toward the table.

. . . or Alvin loves Penelope . . .

He looked down at the pendant.

*. . . or Alistair . . . loves . . . Patricia!
That's it!*

He raced into Jackie's bedroom. In one corner
there was a long table desk cluttered with papers,
recorder tapes, a typewriter, and a large accumulation of newspapers and photographs. Pinned to
the wall above the desk were several pictures of
Patricia Elliot and a *Daily Mirror* front page. It
was the same front page Browning saw in Heaven.

He leaped onto the desk and slid to a halt,
nose-to-nose with the newspaper on the wall. He
looked closer at the picture of Patricia Elliot. It
was there. The pendant was there!

He scrambled across the typewriter to look at
another photograph, then another, and another.
She was wearing the pendant in all of them. In
every picture he saw. He scratched through a
stack of photographs on the desk looking for the
police photograph of the bodies he had seen
earlier.

Did she have it on when I found her?
I don't remember.

Come on, Browning, think!

He strained his memory. Patricia Elliot was on the floor. He bent over her, reaching to check the pulse in her wrist, then her neck. Yes! It was there!

His feet split pictures out of the way like a machine gun, and then it was in front of him. The photograph of their bodies. Patricia's blouse was lying open at the neck . . . and the pendant was not there.

At last. Something.

That means someone took it after I was
killed but before that picture was taken.

He jumped down and began to pace across the room.

The killer. It had to be the killer. And
Bart had possession so that made him it.
Or Alistair Becket himself.

Browning wandered back into the living room, the puzzle pieces scrambling around in his mind.

So Alistair Becket loved Patricia. For at
least a year in Switzerland, is my guess.
Which explains the rumors, the painting,
and the statues. But Alistair had a
family and a political career and Patricia
could ruin both.

Especially since she was engaged to
Becket's number one political opponent.
So poof! No more Patricia.

He stopped and looked toward the coffee table.

But how do I prove it?

He walked back toward the table.

I wonder how Becket would react if a
dog showed up with this thing hanging
out of his mouth.

He stared down at the pendant.

Simple. He'd kill the dog.

He glanced up at the clock above the fireplace.
It was five minutes till noon.

Not if the dog showed up in the middle
of lunch at an elegant French restaurant.

He raced across the room, leaped onto the
chair by the door and pushed the intercom buzzer
with his foot. The doorman's voice crackled
through the speaker.

"Miss Howard?"

Browning barked.

"Oh."

There was a long pause, then a sigh: "I shall
be right up."

Browning jumped down from the chair and
trotted back to the coffee table.

Maybe I should wait and try to get
Jackie involved.

He blinked . . . and picked up the pendant.

Nope. Too dangerous.

A key clicked into the lock and Browning glanced toward the front door.

That was quick.

He trotted across the room preparing himself for the verbal cuffing he knew he would get from the doorman.

Click, click.

Browning waited patiently, the gold pendant dangling from his mouth. Finally the door opened and a jagged blade of fear slashed through every muscle in his body. It wasn't the doorman staring at him. It was Malcolm Bart.

Browning darted through the doorway and Bart spun in pursuit, fumbling for something in his pocket. As he rounded the corner, he careened into the doorman and a large black pistol fell to the floor. For a split second they both stared at it, then Bart picked it up and forced a smile: "You never know these days. What with muggers and all . . ."

He was off down the hall.

Browning raced across the lobby to the front door. It was closed and there was no one around. And no other way out.

At the curb, a chauffeur was helping a tottering elderly lady from a shiny silver Rolls-Royce.

They moved at an agonizingly slow pace toward the door, the chauffeur apparently receiving a list of the day's instructions. Browning glanced anxiously at the stairwell, then back.

Please!!

Browning barked and scratched frantically on the glass, but outside his frenzy couldn't be heard. Only the little old lady.

". . . and then to Harrod's to pick up my brace of pheasants. I must have them for the party. You know how Jonathan loves his pheasants from Harrod's."

The limo driver nodded. "Yes, mum."

"Now, was there anything else?"

Pause.

"I guess not." And finally she turned to the door.

Bart's feet appeared at the top of the stairwell.

The chauffeur opened the door and Browning shot like a streak right between the lady's legs. She stopped to exclaim and Bart almost flattened her as he raced through the doorway.

Browning didn't expect Bart to be in such good shape. He couldn't lose him. He cut through an alley and across a busy street, barely escaping the wheels of a red double decker bus. The bus almost got Bart and he had to wait for it.

This gave Browning a few extra seconds, but he lost them again waiting for a long sheet of plate glass to be carried across the sidewalk by two delivery men. Before he was away, Bart was right back on his heels.

Browning raced up a sidewalk and cut into a courtyard, through a garden, across a parking lot, and out to another driveway exit.

Suddenly he screeched to a halt. Bart had anticipated the move and was standing at the other end waiting for him. Browning spun around and raced back the way he had come . . . with Bart right on his tail.

He decided to try the double-back trick that worked on the big dog. He flew around a corner and dove into the shadows of a big doorway. Bart rounded the corner and came to a screeching halt. He stood for several long moments, his back to Browning, looking from one end of the street to the other. Finally he turned . . . and saw Browning in the shadows. The pendant was still dangling from his mouth.

Well, I guess it comes down to speed versus strength . . .

But suddenly he knew different. He was staring down the barrel of a large automatic pistol. Bart cocked the gun. Now there was no choice. Hoping for a split-second advantage, he picked the gun side of Bart and bolted from the doorway toward the corner.

Bart spun and dove for him and fell in a heap. The gun fired, sending a stray bullet into a barrel

126

of beer which was being wheeled into a pub by a burly delivery man. But Browning was long gone, and Bart raced after him.

Far down the street, Browning cut into a narrow alley between two buildings, then rounded another corner, and suddenly came face-to-face with a dead end.

Great! Now what?

"Now back to Heaven, Mr. Browning."

Browning spun to see Higgins sitting on a trash can. "I'm afraid your time is up."

As before, Browning suddenly found himself back in human form, the pendant still dangling from his mouth. He spit it out.

"I told you before that I'm not going back until I'm through. You sent me down here to do a job and I'm staying until it's finished. Now go work it out!"

Higgins climbed off his trash can. "Mr. Browning, I told you before there's nothing I can do . . ."

He was interrupted by Malcolm Bart rounding the corner on a dead run. He jolted to a stop, eye-to-eye with Browning, and a cold shiver shot up Browning's spine. *Will he remember?*

There was a nervous pause as Bart glanced at the two men. Certainly a suspect group to an even less confused person: one man dressed in white and silver and another in a short, white hospital gown.

Bart glanced back to Browning, looking more like a little boy than an accomplice to a political scandal and murder. He spoke softly.

"Did . . . did . . . a little dog run back here?"

There was another moment of silence and Browning felt the slightest of smiles wrinkle across his face. "Uhh . . . yeah. Sure did. Weirdest thing I've ever seen. Couldn't be a real dog. Came running into this alley, hit that garbage can, went straight up that wall, and just kept going, right into the sky! Like Superman or something!"

Bart stared blankly at the top of the three-story building Browning was pointing to.

"You think I'm crazy, don't you?" Browning hoped he wasn't going too far. "I knew you would. Look, just forget what I said. Don't tell anybody, okay?"

Trancelike, Bart turned and stalked back down the alley.

Browning smiled. "He may never be the same."

"Mr. Browning. There is no more time. Either you come back with me now or . . ."

Browning turned to Higgins.

"Look. Can you guarantee me that everything down here is going to work out if I go back?"

"We don't have that kind of control, Mr. Browning. You know the Doctrine of Free Will. It's a big thing with the Boss."

"Then tell the Boss I'll see him later. There's a guy in jail and a lovely lady depending on a little dog we all know."

He started for the corner. "Now if you'll excuse me, I have a luncheon date."

He put the pendant back in his mouth, then, through clenched teeth: "Woof!"

And he was gone.

Back on the street, a short, cute, fluffy dog raced out of an alley and disappeared around a corner.

23 _____

Chez Revien was a very fashionable outdoor cafe, very French, and very crowded for lunch. It was a London tradition. Year round. A huge canopy kept the rain out and large outdoor heaters kept customers toasty while dining, even in the crisp autumn air.

Jackie and Becket were seated at a table for two near the main traffic pattern, a location which provoked several interruptions in their conversation by well-wishers who recognized the rising young politician.

"You're very popular," Jackie teased.

"You keep saying that."

Becket tasted the wine and approved it. The waiter poured.

"I understand the excitement that must surround the writing of one's first book, but I can't help wondering why you chose this subject."

"Actually, it was my publisher's idea . . ."

Jackie was interrupted by a lady with a napkin and a pen.

"Mr. Becket. Would you mind signing this for my little girl?"

"Not at all."

He signed the napkin.

"Your publisher's idea?"

He signed another napkin.

"Yes, He's a close friend and . . ."

A man passing the table leaned over and patted Beckett on the arm. "Great speech on the tax issue. I'm behind you on every point."

"Thanks, Bob." He turned back to Jackie. "Sorry. So you didn't know Patricia Elliot at all?"

"Never met her."

"Or Quimby Charles?"

"No. Not until I interviewed him after the murders."

Jackie wondered why she felt like she was being grilled. *She* was supposed to ask the questions. She pushed the feeling back and continued. "Anyway, my publisher has said for years that he was going to do this for me when the right subject came along. Something really commercial. For him it's topical and has sex appeal. For me, it seems to be about really interesting people."

"But if you didn't know the people, how did you know they would be . . ."

Becket stopped in mid-sentence. He was staring across the table at Browning who was peering at him through the salad. The pendant dangled from his mouth.

Becket's face went white. "What's that?!"

Jackie looked down. "Where did you come from?? Where did you get this?"

She took the pendant from Browning and held it up by the ends of the chain. Becket's eyes flashed and he struck out, snatching it away.

"Indeed! I suspected as much!"

"I beg your pardon."

"The big prize! Get Alistair Becket. He's getting too close to the top. Show no mercy."

He looked up at Jackie. "How much are they paying you?"

Jackie was dumbfounded.

"Who? What . . ."

Becket didn't wait for an answer.

"What kind of person does this with someone else's life?"

Jackie looked down at the tape recorder in her lap. Browning was punching the *record* button with his paw. He looked up and their eyes met.

Contact!

Jackie didn't believe what she was thinking! And there was no time to think about what she was believing.

"You certainly have no compassion. And no integrity. The little games you played." Becket mimicked Jackie: "What was Patricia Elliot really like? What drove Patricia Elliot? What were her great passions?"

People in the area were beginning to stare.

Becket leaned across the table.

"Why didn't you have the guts to say what you knew, instead of sneaking around, picking up the edges to see if I'd crack!"

Becket glared at Jackie for a long moment, but she had nothing to say. Truly nothing. He sighed and sank back into his chair, his look shifting to the pendant. He turned it over and gazed intently at the inscription. Tears began to form.

"It's true you know. It wasn't playtime. I really loved her."

Then it all rushed into Jackie's head at once. The shock, the realization. She began pushing her chair backward.

"You killed her." It was almost a whisper.

Becket looked up. "What??" Then he realized what she had said. "No . . ."

"You killed her!" Jackie was louder now. "You killed Patricia Elliot!"

Panic flickered in Becket's eyes as he glanced around at the staring faces.

"No . . ."

"Yes!"

"No, Miss Howard!" It was a new voice.

Jackie spun to see Bart standing near the table with both hands in his pockets. He was pale and drained, washed of emotion.

"Alistair didn't kill Patricia. I did."

Becket reacted in shock. "What??!"

Bart seemed calm at first, without feeling, but as he talked a poisoned intensity began to consume him.

"I had to. I had spent twelve years getting you ready, and Patricia Elliot would have ruined everything."

He walked over to Becket.

"One word to Quimby Charles about Switzerland and we'd be through, you and I. If word got out that you and she were . . . I couldn't let that happen. You *will* be Prime Minister. England needs you. It was all too important. And it was all perfect . . ." His icy stare turned and penetrated Browning. ". . . If it hadn't been for that dog!"

In the distance the maitre d' was leading two policemen toward the table. Bart took the pendant from Becket and gazed at it, glassy-eyed.

"This was my souvenir. In case you ever doubted my loyalty or my value to you. It was safely put away in a post office box . . . until . . ."

Bart looked at Browning, his eyes blank and empty, yet at the same time, totally possessed.

"He's the devil, you know. He came here to stop us, you and me, from being Prime Minister. He stopped me but he won't you. He won't stop anything anymore."

His pocket moved and a gun appeared.

Jackie screamed: "No!" And she swooped down to shield Browning.

Crack!

The sound of the gunshot rang through the restaurant and Jackie's face froze for a split second, then dropped lifeless to the floor.

Oh no! No . . . no . . . no . . .

Two policemen grabbed Bart and separated him from his gun, then attempted to calm the erupting chaos.

Browning heard none of it. He just felt a pain, sharper, deeper, even than the night he was murdered. In raw agony, he crumpled into a heap next to Jackie's body and nuzzled his head under her chin . . . and his tear-filled eyes began to overflow.

No . . . no . . . no.

24

It was a dismal foggy morning by the Thames. Browning was miserable. For a day and a night he had moped forlornly from nowhere to nowhere. Alone, lost, not caring. Not eating, not sleeping. He saw her face and heard her voice with every step.

He paused to glance at a cat sitting on a newspaper vending rack and wished it was a Returnable. He'd like someone to talk to.

Below the cat, bold headlines screamed off the newspaper page, raking across his memory:

QUIMBY CHARLES CLEARED!

BECKET ASSISTANT CHARGED!

NOVELIST MURDERED!

A picture of Jackie accompanied the headlines

but it was a Jackie from years ago. Much younger than . . . yesterday. Browning looked away and walked off.

"Lousy picture, don't you think?"

Browning spun around and looked everywhere. It was Jackie's voice. He had heard Jackie's voice.

But there was no one in sight. Nothing but an empty bench, a newspaper rack, and a cat.

>*I can't stand it! Now I'm hearing her voice.*

He turned and walked to the edge of the river.

"For Pete's sake, don't jump!"

Browning spun around again. Still no one. Nothing. Except . . . the glint of something metal around the cat's neck. He took a few steps closer. It was! A Returnable tag!

>*Jackie??*

The cat turned and looked him square in the eye.

>*Benjamin Browning. Nice to meet you, officially, that is.*

Browning did a flip in the air.

>*I don't believe it!*

Jackie jumped down to face Browning and he gazed into her eyes. Not quite the same body, but the same eyes. Big, brown, and beautiful. She was black-and-gray striped with a soft white patch under her throat and four white feet. And her eyes were incredible.

> *Why did you come back?*

Jackie turned and strolled down the sidewalk and Browning followed.

> *I wasn't about to let you be the martyr in this situation. You stayed down here for me so the least I could do was come back and keep you company. And none too soon. A fine mess you would have left me in if you had jumped in the river.*

> *Oh, I never would have done that. I'm a coward at heart.*

Jackie paused to slap playfully at a falling leaf, then walked on.

> *Well, now that we're on the same level, so to speak, what do you want me to call you? Benjamin, BJ, or what?*

> *Not Benjamin. I hate it. BJ . . . or some of my friends used to call me Benji.*

She stopped and looked him up and down.

> *Better stick with BJ. You're not the Benji type.*

The first rays of morning sun broke through the mist and fell softly on the walkway before them, accompanied quite appropriately, Browning thought, by a faint and distant heavenly chorus. Synthesized, and probably computerized, but heavenly nonetheless.

It was going to be a good day.

Woof.